JANE GILLEY was born in Nottingham and now lives on the beautiful island of Jersey with her husband, a rabbit and a Senegal parrot. Following a career in Interior Design, she now writes full-time.

JANE GILLEY

The Woman Who Kept Everything

avon.

A division of HarperCollins*Publishers*

www.harpercollins.co.uk

Published by AVON
A division of HarperCollins*Publishers* Ltd
1 London Bridge Street
London SE1 9GF

www.harpercollins.co.uk

This paperback edition 2019

1

First published in Great Britain by
HarperCollins*Publishers* 2018

A catalogue copy of this book is available
from the British Library.

ISBN: 978-0-00-830863-6

This novel is entirely a work of fiction. The names, characters and
incidents portrayed in it are the work of the author's imagination. Any
resemblance to actual persons, living or dead, events or localities is
entirely coincidental.

Typeset in Birka by Palimpsest Book Production Limited,
Falkirk, Stirlingshire
Printed and bound in UK by
CPI Group (UK) Ltd, Croydon CR0 4YY

MIX
Paper from
responsible sources
FSC™ C007454

The Woman
Who Kept
Everything

Chapter 1

The boiling hot water splashed over Gloria's fingers.
'Waargh!'

She did a little agony dance whilst she waited for the pain to ease, blowing on her fingers. Damn. She'd need to get outside to dunk her hand in the cold water barrel.

Her oldest friend, Tilsbury, was always harping on about that darned pan; said that using it, without a lid, instead of a kettle, might prove disastrous one day. Gloria wouldn't buy a kettle, though. Said she didn't have the money for expensive items like that. Well, her son, Clegg, had given her a credit card for 'essential items' but she never went anywhere to use it. In fact, she rarely went out at all. She didn't really need to.

Today she'd knocked the pan by accident, reaching over to check the potato soup she was cooking for their lunch. These days she was always eating potato soup, on account that she had a large sack of them, out back, that Tilsbury had got from someone *in the know*. She liked that it could be a cheap nourishing meal when she had onions, carrots and a good stock in it.

But, today, she only had potatoes. Add a bit of salt and it

would have to do, she'd thought. Anyway, the hot water for their tea, boiling away in the pan next to the soup, had sploshed onto her left hand as she'd leaned over the grimy stove to stir their meal.

Gloria grunted as she hitched up her Crimplene dress and clambered over the piles of squashed cardboard boxes and magazines, nearly slipping on mouldy teabags, decomposing potato skins, marmalade-smeared crusts and other detritus around the kitchen sink unit. She no longer noticed the stink like rotting cabbage. Empty, dripping or congealed milk cartons, plastic bags and other household rubbish also littered the floor – more obstacles to tackle – in order to get to that cold water barrel, outside by the back door. The original Georgian taps in her kitchen sink had long since seized up. So the only water she could use was in that rainwater barrel, outdoors: for cooking, for occasional washing, for everything really.

But, at seventy-nine, she knew she was getting too old for all this.

Her fingers were blistered from similar events. A kettle would make things easier, of course. But it wasn't just the money. She felt pretty much housebound now, more from lack of motivation and despondency than anything else. There wasn't anything physically preventing her from doing things. She occasionally forgot things but she wasn't an invalid and she didn't need to use a walking stick yet, even though she was a bit wobbly on her feet sometimes. So she could go down to the shops if she wanted. She just didn't want to, any more. Anyway, Tilsbury would pop by and get her the things she really needed, when she needed anything.

'Go fetch us a tub of marge,' she'd say to Tilsbury, when he came round to see what else she needed before he went to fetch her pension for her. 'Bit of honey wouldn't go amiss, either. And get me a bar of that Imperial Leather soap. I likes that, for a treat, I do.'

So Tilsbury, duly, got all the bits she needed from the corner shop and collected her pension as well. And her son, Clegg, got her teabags, carrots, eggs and bread, when he remembered to come see her. He hadn't been to see her in a while, though. Three weeks four days, to be precise, Gloria noted, missing him. She crossed the white squares off on the calendar board attached to the back of the door – the calendar board Tilsbury had made and put up for her – in between her son's sporadic visits. She counted the days until he reappeared at her door, hopefully with another bag of groceries or provisions in hand.

When her husband, Arthur, was alive it hadn't been a problem. Clegg had even brought the rest of the family around to visit as well. Oh, it'd been lovely seeing little Jessie and Adam, her only grandchildren. But since Clegg had told her he'd got busier and busier at work he'd been coming to see her less and less. And she hadn't seen the children or his wife, Val, in – what? Crikey, yes, at least ten years or more. Such a shame, such a real shame, Gloria thought sadly.

Once, though, Tilsbury had tried to cuff Clegg, after

listening to Gloria moan for years about the way her son treated her. Tilsbury told Clegg he was a useless bastard for the way he allowed his mother to live in this dump of a place, rarely visiting. But Clegg was a bulky gruff of a man and had thumped Tilsbury instead. 'Phaww. That stung a bit, it did, my love,' he'd whimpered to Gloria, who'd merely shaken her head. So Tilsbury kept out of the way when Clegg visited now.

Gloria and Tilsbury went *way* back. From school, initially.

Oh, those were the days, Gloria often thought, even though there was such a lot of clearing up and rebuilding being done after the Second World War. But she remembered being quite shy as a youngster, probably because she was an only child and adopted. Her adoptive mum, Alice, was a kind but childless woman who made sure Gloria was loved and she doted on her as though she was her own blood. At primary school she'd only had two friends: Jocelyn and Mabel. And her favourite thing, she remembered, was playing in the school sandpit with them or seeing who could do the best handstand. They'd also gone to secondary school together and it was there they met Tilsbury, and his friends – a group of boys who were a year older than them.

Gloria clicked with him immediately because of his ease around girls and they started seeing each other. He'd walk her home from school or she'd drag Jocelyn along to watch him play footie at weekends. At one point, though, she nearly fell out with Jocelyn who also said she fancied him.

However, Tilsbury then went to India with his family for a good few years because his father was a rail track engineer. When they all came back he took up with Gloria again but couldn't settle and didn't seem to know what he wanted out of life. He decided to leave Norwich in his late teens to 'find out what I want to do', he said.

So Gloria had decided to forget about him and move on with her life. Mabel got married and had children, early on, to Gerard – a boy-next-door type – and Jocelyn and Gloria got jobs as secretaries and enjoyed themselves as single young women. Eventually Gloria got together with Arthur, a reliable and honourable young man who worked for a manufacturing company and was liked by everyone. She met him at a barn dance.

When Tilsbury returned to the area after his travels around the country he married Jocelyn, much to Gloria's surprise. In those early days it did cause a bit of a rift between them all. Jocelyn hadn't dared tell Gloria who she was going out with at first. 'Well, you were with Arthur. And it just 'appened!' she ruefully admitted to Gloria, later. But they'd been good friends and the rift healed, eventually, and they resumed a friendship of sorts. Besides Gloria had her life with Arthur and they had their young son, Clegg, and they were very happy.

And then many years later, Tilsbury started dropping by every few weeks, helping Gloria out with errands or a bit of DIY, when her husband Arthur died, in the Nineties. But it tickled Gloria to think that Tilsbury had always been sweet on her.

'Just keeping an eye out for you, old girl,' he'd say.

'I'm middle-aged, you oaf, not ancient yet! Besides I don't need you always fussing round me,' she'd told him, huffily. 'Go fuss round your own family.'

What family?

His estranged wife Jocelyn had shooed him out of their cramped council house, years earlier, after he'd tripped over another one of her flippin' rescue cats. She swore he'd kicked it. *He hadn't!* He'd said the house felt overcrowded – not because they'd ever had kids but because there'd been a constant flow of ruddy cats in the place, nineteen at last count. Some had bits missing from their ears; one had no ears. Some were flea-ridden; some pregnant or scrawny. And there was fur and faeces trays everywhere. Meow, meow, meow, all day long, and then howling at night. It annoyed the neighbours; *it drove him crazy.* It was a bloody madhouse. Anyway, Jocelyn – in no uncertain terms – told him to leave but he knew he was best off out of it.

'I'm gone,' were his last words as he left without a final nod to his wife.

So Tilsbury dossed in the park when it was warm enough and bagged a bed wherever he could the rest of the time – mainly at the shelter, occasionally at his sister's or with friends. His life remained like that for quite a while. No responsibility for anyone or anything was how he decided he liked it best.

However, Tilsbury was thoroughly annoyed when Jocelyn moved on – and with his brother, Marvin, to boot! Previously they'd all been good friends, in the same clique. Miffed, Tilsbury had, on occasion, slipped into their house, when he knew they were safely down the dogs and nicked a bit of their rent money or topped up his hip flask with their vodka. He justified it by thinking it was the very least they could do after the way they'd treated him. And it kept him going each month when funds and sympathy were tight.

Besides, he reasoned, why would they always leave their spare key in the same place? It was his old hiding spot and they knew he was still around.

And – oh, yes – they'd always gotten mad with him, if they caught him when they got back, especially if he was making a sandwich or having a cup of tea. But a 'Piss off, bruv' from Marvin usually sent him scampering.

But finally, after years of Tilsbury's periodic comings and goings and helping her out at her own house, Gloria felt sorry for him and said he could stay at hers, on those occasions when he didn't otherwise have anywhere else to go.

'Right now, my dear. If you wants to kip here for the night, whenever you needs to, you can. But it won't be first class at the Hilton, you understand, because you might just notice I'm not too fussy about me housekeepin'. Ha, ha. Now the downside is that the only bit of room I've got free is right here in the hall. If we shift these boxes a bit more towards the kitchen, you can squeeze in down there.'

So Tilsbury had rooted around upstairs and found a couple of blankets and plonked them on the floor over a wodge of newspapers. Reckoned it kept him warm enough, the nights he stayed – even in the winter – and so they got on like that.

Gloria often told Tilsbury she wished she'd got a house with 'all mod cons' like she'd seen on the telly – when she'd had a telly. Well, she still had a telly but she wasn't quite sure where it was now. Least there wasn't the darned licence to pay for any more.

Anyway, she knew her television was somewhere in the room that used to be a lounge. And it probably still was a lounge under all the masses of stuff in there. But there were masses of stuff everywhere, now. It rose up around her like huge towers, locking her in. It made her feel safe. But Gloria certainly knew – oh, she could *see* – that her house was a humongous mess. But she had neither the strength nor resolve to even *begin* the colossal task of sorting it all out now.

'Too late for all that, dearie,' she'd say when someone made a derogatory comment. 'It has to stay in here, ducks! Where else can it all go?'

Chapter 2

Even though Gloria realised what a state her house was in, she'd felt very blessed and privileged that her *real* family had left her this house. What a bonus! Number 75 Briar Way handed to her on a plate, it was. And no siblings to share it with either; just Arthur, when he was alive. It had been fantastic being able to escape the constant struggle to find money, each month, for their council tenancy. Getting their own real, proper house was like a dream come true for them.

'And one less chuffin' worry,' Arthur used to say.

She recalled how her real ma and pa had left her the house. Well, actually, her grandmother had left it to her. She'd gotten a letter from her grandmother's solicitor, years ago, along with the deeds to her house. She and Arthur were living in a scantily furnished council house, with their young son, whilst they tried to save up for better things. The letter also explained why she'd been given up for adoption.

Hello my darling Gloria,

Let me introduce myself. I am your grandmother, Barbara, and the purpose of my letter today is to explain some things for you.

I'm leaving my house to you in my Will on my death. As well as my house – which would have fallen to your parents on my death, and then to yourself, anyway – I wish to explain why you were not brought up by myself, following the untimely deaths of your beloved parents. I have also enclosed a couple of photographs: one of myself at a party and one of your parents' wedding, outside the church. That's me to the right of your mother.

Anyway, when you were a baby, the bombs started dropping on Britain at the outbreak of World War II. Your father, Walter, was working in the mustard factory and your mother – my only daughter, Emily – was a domestic cleaner. They were living with me in my house, whilst they saved up for their own family home. But en route to a rare evening out with friends, they both died tragically, in a bombing raid in Norwich, in July of 1940.

A couple of earlier bombing sessions had struck buildings and there'd been no fatalities. But on that particular night there'd been no air raid warning, either, as there sometimes wasn't, and a lot of other mustard factory workers lost their lives that night too.

However, it was very fortunate your mother and father had chosen to leave you at home with me, that evening. I managed the daily procedures quite well at first, despite the problems that regular bombing raids brought, as well as food shortages. I even managed to find you a wet nurse. But, unfortunately, I couldn't cope with a tiny baby by myself on account of my arthritis, which has always been a problem for me. I also didn't want to be evacuated, so I had to make the difficult decision to have you adopted by a sweet woman I knew, Alice McKensie, who lived outside the city. (As my arthritis has recently got much worse, this letter is being transcribed by someone else.)

However, I kept in touch with Alice, your adoptive mother, and told her you'd inherit my house, on my death, when you were ready to take possession of it and as long as it wasn't bombed during the war. She often let me know how you were doing and sent me photos.

So I truly hope you can forgive my giving you up and I hope that my gift of the house will help ease any financial burdens you might possibly have in the future. I sincerely hope you live a long and very happy existence, my darling.

Your ever-loving grandmother
Barbara xxxxx

'Of course, I forgive you, dear grandmother,' Gloria had whispered to the letter, as tears had flowed, unheeded, down her face. 'It was war. It wasn't ordinary circumstances. And at least I know my family history now.'

Her adopted mum, Alice, had always been a loving, encouraging person, so Gloria knew she hadn't missed out by not having the chance to be brought up by her own parents. And she'd been thrilled with the life-changing gift of a house, which'd come at a time when Arthur had lost his job through a back injury and they *had* been struggling with their finances.

* * *

Gloria couldn't actually remember when she'd started collecting things.

She'd always loved going to car boots for bargains. But after her beloved adopted mum died, Arthur had cleared out her council house – putting most of Alice's things in their large shed out back. Gloria hadn't wanted to get rid of Alice's stuff. It made her feel like she still had her mother with her but it seemed to kick-start her collecting with a vengeance and she'd started bringing more and more stuff back from everywhere. Mainly from car boot sales but sometimes she found paraphernalia on roads outside people's houses. They were a scruffy lot, she said, leaving three-legged chairs, old duvets or broken toys and other stuff just lying around, littering the streets.

But Arthur had gone wild about it.

'Here, Glor, what're you doing with all that stuff and all them house magazines? You don't even like *Changing Rooms*.'

When Gloria had ignored his questioning, he'd tried a more gentle approach.

'Yes but how much of this stuff do you really need and what do you need it for, my love?'

And when that hadn't worked, he'd found himself close to tipping point.

'Gloria, this's got to stop! It's in every room and I don't want anything else in the lounge. Can't see the telly! This place isn't big enough for all this ruddy clobber.'

However Gloria had the 'bug' now and it was a very hard habit to break.

'Never know when we might need some of it, though, Arth!'

Yet when Arthur got ill and his heart gave out to obesity, the hoarding just went on and on, increasing in intensity; increasing in the never-ending storing of items Gloria knew she had no intention of using or mending. But insisted she *needed*.

Due to the resistance she'd encountered because of the way she'd lived these past twenty years, Gloria knew folk didn't understand why she needed to have lots of things around her. They didn't know of her heartache when her adoptive mum died, nor how distraught she'd been when Arthur died. Distraught, especially when Arthur died because Clegg seemed to pull away from her after that. Perhaps it was the male influence he missed now Arthur was no longer here.

But it was as though, suddenly, there was no one around her who loved her and no one around her who *she* could love. No one was there with a friendly word or even those delicious little hugs from the grandchildren, when they'd been allowed to visit. And Arthur wasn't there with that cup of tea he brought her, at the end of the day, and his: 'Sleep tight, love, don't let the bed bugs bite.'

So Gloria realised that having things around her made her feel safe when there was no one else around her to make her feel that way. It was almost as though she'd created walls to protect herself, she thought. Yet these walls were made from magazines or old boxes. Yes, that's how she'd describe it. But even though Tilsbury had tried to make her see how alienated everyone else felt about what she was doing, she simply couldn't bring herself to *stop* doing it.

The only room relatively free from junk was the bathroom now. It was always quite an arduous trip to get into the bathroom and even when she was there, the bath was stacked high with newspapers so she couldn't use that any more. But at least she could wash in the sink, if she wanted, and use the loo. Or at least she *could* use them, after she'd stumbled over knick-knacks cluttering the stairs. *And* climbing over unruly piles of old clothing, including all Clegg's baby clothes, which she'd kept in case she'd had more babies (unfortunately, it hadn't happened) and heaps of towels and surplus carpet rolls, which she'd kept in case the carpet wore out.

Tilsbury said he didn't mind the state of the place, though. Said it made the place warmer, cosier somehow.

'Saves on washing and cleaning and all that crazy shite.'

But the following day there was a loud bang when Gloria turned one of the hob rings on and tried to heat the remaining potato soup from yesterday. The small kitchen was quickly filled with the nasty smell of something burning.

Tilsbury was hopping around in mild terror.

'Ooo, my love! You gotta get the electricity people out now. Could be a fire! You insured?'

'Wouldn't know, Tils. Never really pay for anything any more, do I, ducks. S'all set up out of me bank account or summat. Cleggy sorted it all out for me after Arthur went, as you know. But I can smell summat singeing! Get hold of me son for me, will ya, ducks? Cleggy'll sort it all out. Bit worried about being burned alive in my bed. You hear of it happening.'

Chapter 3

A few days after the people from the electricity board came to check on the situation, three people from social services turned up; one with a clipboard. They looked official, to Gloria, with their curt smiles and long dark coats. She would've said they were calm and sympathetic, if someone'd asked. But they didn't look that way after their first encounter with 75 Briar Way.

They came into her house, sniffing the air and gagging for some reason. One of them, a man, ran out muttering something. Gloria found it amusing. Tilsbury went round shrugging.

'Must've eaten summat off before they came here.'

The plump, friendlier woman who finally arrived later that first day, Diane, was the most understanding, but even *she* had a strongly scented handkerchief she kept wafting across her face. Gloria screwed her nose up at the smell and stood a little distance away from her. She wasn't keen on heavy perfumes.

Oh, but there was nowhere to sit per se. That was the tricky thing about having more than one person over at any one time. And in order to be courteous, Tilsbury had to clamber over a lot of stuff, upstairs, to get the stool off the top of Gloria's bedside dressing table, so Diane could sit down in the tiny bit of space between the hall and kitchen door. Gloria leant against the architrave and rested her burnt hand on a stack of crumpled magazines.

Now that Diane had finished looking around – her mouth gaping in awe, her handkerchief not far from her nose – she said that her mother had been just like Gloria when Diane's grandparents died. Couldn't quite accept it; still didn't; in a nursing home now.

'Much better for her. All her woes dealt with and she's *properly* cared for.'

Gloria didn't really know what the woman was talking about. She wasn't interested to know something about someone she didn't know and would never know and, anyway, her hand ached. She grimaced as she tried to reposition it.

'Oh my, that hand looks sore, love. Should've wrapped it in cling film or something clean if you had it. But, anyway, don't you worry about all that, now. We've got to get you away from here and do some sorting out,' Diane informed her, with a bright smile.

Gloria shook her head solemnly. 'Don't want to go anywhere else. Been here so many years, ducks, and I certainly don't want to go anywhere now.'

'I know that, Gloria! But we've, um, we've got to sift through all this – er – this stuff to try and find where the electrics blew. Your house's become a bit of a fire hazard now, so we're taking you somewhere safe while we sort things out. And that hand of yours needs looking at.'

Clegg appeared at that precise moment, his large frame filling the already clogged front doorway. He was sweating and also trying not to gag. He squeezed past them to try and look at the kitchen, pushing boxes and piles of magazines aside in his attempt to get through, but then he stopped, deciding against it.

'Oh stuff this! Right, Mum. Bleeerr. God! What a stench! And what on earth is all that crap and rubbish doing over there by the kitchen sink? Wasn't there last time I came. Good grief, there's bits of food in it as well, Mother! What on earth've you been doing?'

'I think some hooligans nicked me wheelie-bin, Cleggy. So I leave me household rubbish near the back door. Can't put it outside. Foxes might get it!'

Clegg gagged and put his hand over his mouth, shaking his head.

'Un-fucking-believable! Right, well, I got rid of that bloody scoundrel, Tilsbury. Seems to me he's using your ruddy good nature to wheedle his way into favour, rent-free, and how's that helpin' matters? It ain't, Mother. So you're coming with me. And I don't want any more ruddy arguments. Plus it's not safe for you in here with all this crap everywhere and dodgy electrics.'

He turned his back on his mother and nodded to Diane.

'Just get rid of the bloody LOT! Don't care how you do it

but just DO it. Give me any paperwork you find in drawers and the like but otherwise there's nowt of any value. I'll pay for what needs payin' for but just get rid of it. And, er, thanks for getting her a place at Green's Nursin' Home for a couple of weeks. They'll clean her up and sort her out a treat, I'm told,' he said through clenched teeth.

'They certainly will, Mr Frensham. They're one of the best homes in the district. And you say you're happy to take her afterwards? Is that for full-time care or will you need some additional help?' mumbled Diane, behind her handkerchief.

Clegg shook his head vehemently. 'No. We'll be okay with that, thanks. My Val's sorting all that side out. She's a nurse as you know. We've got a small en suite extension for my mother. So we'll all be fine at home together. God! That smell is unbearable! Dunno how she's put up with it all these years. Nowt so queer as folk, as they say.'

Chapter 4

From the moment Gloria stepped foot inside Green's Nursing Home she decided she didn't like it.

Well, it wasn't 75 Briar Way, for one thing! And where were her belongings? Where was her winceyette nightie? Where was her splayed blue toothbrush for cleaning her dentures with? And where was her little alarm clock with no battery that Arthur bought her, back in the day, which she kept under her pillow when she slept? She liked those things around her. They brought her comfort.

Clegg had driven her to the nursing home. His wife Val was not with him and nor were the children. Gloria felt as though she was being shuttled away somewhere, out of everyone's hair.

'Right, Mother. I've got to go. Already had more time off work than is good for me. You go in through those doors, there, to reception and ask for Mrs Lal. She'll be looking after you,' he'd said, revving his engine. Once Gloria had clambered out, he'd driven off without so much as a wave. Gloria shook her head. Clegg's behaviour was not what it used to be.

The lady who'd met Gloria in reception, Mrs Lal, was the

chief carer. She'd asked if Gloria would like a brief tour first but all Gloria wanted to do was squirrel herself away and have a jolly good think about things. Plus she wasn't good at speaking to new people because she hadn't had to do that for a long time.

So Mrs Lal had taken Gloria upstairs via a lift and showed her into a very small room with a single bed, one chair and a wardrobe and nothing else at all. No 'things' or 'stuff'. The décor was insipid. Pale peach walls, pale peach bedspread. Pale this, pale that. Not the mish-mash of colours, textures and chaos she was used to. Gloria felt downhearted. Clegg had told her she'd be here for two weeks while he sorted things out with the house. So she knew she had no choice but to stay and accept this place and the people she found within its walls.

Clothes, not new ones, had been left on the bed for her to change into. They weren't her own. Mrs Lal had shown her where the shower and toilet were and asked her to have a good shower and hair wash with the gels provided.

'You okay with that, Mrs Frensham, or do you need someone to help you get cleaned up?' Mrs Lal had said with a kindly smile.

The very thought had appalled Gloria, that someone might have to clean her one day. It would not be today, however. She had shaken her head so hard that she thought it might fall off.

'No, ducks. I don't want touchin' by no one, ta very much.'

Mrs Lal had said she understood and then told Gloria she was to come downstairs after her shower and she'd be shown where she would have dinner and eat all her meals.

Gloria was a little damp when she finally found her way back to the reception area. In fact, she'd been in the shower so long, just enjoying the sensation of hot water cascading over her, for the first time in twenty years, that dinner had finished and the only food the cook could prepare was a cold chicken salad with two slices of white buttered bread.

But Gloria tucked in hungrily, thinking it was probably the best meal she'd ever tasted. It certainly beat potato soup! And then, feeling completely shattered, she asked if she could go to bed.

Mrs Lal took her back upstairs to her room afterwards and Gloria lay on top of the soft bed, fully clothed, staring at the ceiling. There was a light switch by the bed so she could switch the light off whenever she wanted. But Gloria spent a good couple of hours just staring at the Artexed ceiling, wondering where they were going to put all her things whilst they searched for the electricity fault. And how would they know where to put her things back afterwards? And would the house she'd lived in for thirty-some-odd years ever be the same again, when everyone had finished poking around in it? She felt a tear prickling the corner of her eye and wiped it away. Clegg would sort it all out for her, she was sure. But his behaviour, she'd noted of late, was becoming alarmingly discourteous.

The next day Mrs Lal came to fetch her and took her to breakfast. She was put on a table with two other white-haired ladies: Yvonne and Annie. They didn't say much. In fact, Gloria wondered if there was something wrong with them. They just seemed to stare ahead without any knowledge of what was going on around them. A carer had to place toast in front of them and encourage them to eat. One man on another table suddenly shrieked, which made Gloria jump.

Gloria got up and went to find Mrs Lal and told her what had been going on.

'Summat's not right with Dotty and Lotty, love. And there's a poor man in anguish over t'other side. Think summat needs to be done about them.'

Gloria could see Mrs Lal was trying to stifle a chuckle.

'Oh, Gloria. I'd forgot you're not used to the daily comings and goings in a nursing home, are you. Well there are some people here who need a lot of care, you see. And there's others like yourself who are just, um, visiting for a short while. Yvonne and Annie are sisters and they've both had strokes so they need a certain amount of help and care. We sat you next to them because they're very quiet. They're not like Henry who does have a tendency to shout a bit. And some of the others can't get used to new people straight away. So that's why we put you there. If you'd prefer to be on your own, of course, we can set a separate table up for you for the duration of your stay.'

Gloria shook her head. 'No, that's all right. They don't make no fuss. And you've explained things to me now. So I under-stands, I do.'

After breakfast Mrs Lal led Gloria into a beautiful light and airy pale green room with trailing plants, an aquarium and bamboo seating and introduced her to Kate, a social worker, who said she was going to have some regular general chats with Gloria, whilst she was here, to find out what she'd been doing since her husband's demise.

By the second day Gloria was looking forward to her next conversational session with Kate. It had been a long time since she'd had meaningful chats with anyone. In fact she usually only saw the postman, Tilsbury, Clegg occasionally, and a persistent window cleaner who reckoned her windows needed more than a simple hose-down – cheeky git. Plus she was starting to get used to her tiny characterless bedroom, now, and she'd even gotten a chuckle or two out of Yvonne and Annie.

Chapter 5

'Cup of tea, Gloria! I'll put it on the table. No, don't worry about your hand. That shaking comes and goes, I know. Least your sores have been treated. And I like your hair now they've cut it. It's much better shaped like that, instead of long and straggly, don't you think?' said Val. 'You must be feeling much better in yourself now everything's been sorted out? That nursing home did wonders for you!'

Gloria didn't look at Val. Her mouth was full of Victoria sponge, anyway. But she had nothing to say to the daughter-in-law she hadn't seen in ten years.

'I'll leave you to look out the window then. The garden's nice this time of year isn't it? Nice to look at.'

Val left the conservatory, closing the door behind her quietly, shaking her head slowly. She looked tired. There were grey bags under her eyes, belying her forty-eight years, flecks of grey, also, in her short dark hair; her fringe was clipped back with a hairgrip. Clegg beckoned her into the kitchen.

'She *never* acknowledges anything I say to her, Cleggy. Just stares ahead. I get the feeling she either wants to hit me or spit.'

Clegg pulled Val into a tight hug and kissed her cheek. 'It's just her way, love. Look – hey! Are you regrettin' this now? We spoke about this at length, din't we? She'd've never left that place unless summat serious happened and thank God it did, in a way.'

Val pulled away from him, leant back against the sink and crossed her arms.

'But I don't think I can stand any more of this silent treatment. It's only been a couple of weeks. And we can't keep the kids away forever. Adam says he can't concentrate on his studying whilst he's over at Zac's. He says they're partying all the time, instead of studying – don't laugh, Cleggy! He's just not into partying like his mates, is he? At least he'll get a decent job at the end of the day. Plus, I've heard Zac's probably taking stuff. So I want them back home. And your mum should be in a home or summat – she really should!'

Val shook her head when Clegg wouldn't meet her gaze. She loaded the dishwasher with their lunch things, then poured their tea and sat down at the table, contemplating her husband as he sipped his hot drink.

'Look, Clegg, I know we talked about all this but *are* we doin' the right thing here?'

'Yes I think we are, Val. Look. I know she's annoyin'. And – hell – she's agile for seventy-nine! So, yes, she could possibly go on livin' for another twenty years or so – there's longevity in the family. But, like I keep tellin' you, we simply *can't* afford to put her into a nursin' home, just yet. We haven't got that sort of money, as you well know. Somewhere down the line, of course, we'll find somewhere for her to go because there's no way she's livin' with us full-time. But you just have to be patient a little while longer.'

When Val didn't respond, he took hold of his wife's hand. 'Can't we just give it a go?'

Val pulled her hand away and cut him a slice of her Victoria sponge. He took it and wolfed it down in two bites.

She looked at him thoughtfully. 'Not even with the sale of her house?'

'What? Well no, Val! Not even with the sale of her house! There'd be virtually nothing left out of the proceeds if we used that to pay her nursing home bills! It's more than £24,000 a year just to keep her alive in those places, as you well know. And we don't have that sort of money to pay for it. So no, Val. The proceeds from the sale of her house are going to benefit all of us! *Like I keep telling you*. We want to retire early, don't we, as well as put the kids through uni? All those things cost a lot of money that we simply don't have on either of our wages. And I, for one, can't wait to get out of the security business. You know I'm fed up with being a security guard. It's boring and the hours are crap. That's why we're doin' all this, isn't it? If her house is worth what we think it is then there should be something in it for all of us – even Mum when the time comes to put her in an old peoples' home. Hopefully, she'll see sense, about all of this, and then happily sign on the dotted line and that'll be that.'

Val slapped the table, which made her husband jump.

'Look, do you really think she's just going to say, "Well, here's the money from the house, Cleggy?" You're mad if you do. I've seen how stubborn she gets, remember? Your poor dad, having to put up with all that junk brought into the house over the years. There was no room to breathe let alone live in. And remember the time we tried to help her? Took us days, remember? We cleared everything out and cleaned the house and put it all outside for the bin-men to take away and then she just dragged it all back in because she said it looked *scruffy* outside on the kerb! And that time Jessie fell. Well, the house is a ruddy danger zone too. The whole thing's bloody crazy, if you ask me. And I'm an easy-going sort of person. Bottom line, though, Cleggy, she's not going to simply roll over and die, whatever you might hope for.'

Clegg growled.

'All right! I *know* she's bloody stubborn, Val. But look at it this way – I'm her only son, so it's all comin' to me one way or another. Oh, don't look at me like that, Val! Me and Mum have never really got on over the years, have we? We've *tolerated* each other, at best. So you don't ever have to worry about her being a permanent fixture in our household. Plus you know I've only ever thought about us and the kids the whole way through this. I've had to put my own family first, especially since there was nothing more we could do to stop her hoarding. You can only do so much for someone. But that electrical fault – halleluiah – that was the icin' on the cake, as far as I'm concerned! So I really do think that *now* she'll see sense when I mention the uni bills for Adam and Jessie. She'll want them to finish their education properly. She'll want to help us out, Val. I'm sure of it.'

'But it's *me* who'll be looking after her, Cleggy.'

'Yes but not for long, sweetheart! Mebbe a year or so. Then we can put her away somewhere. She's in the annexe, out of our hair, anyway. She's got her own TV and things in there. She won't be under our feet all the time. So it really shouldn't be a problem. You'll cope, Val. You're a ruddy nurse for God's sake; it shouldn't be so difficult for you. Isn't that why we planned this?'

Val shook her head again. 'Yeah but at least with my patients I get to come home and have a rest. This is going to be full on, day in, day out. And what if she decides not to speak to me at all?'

'Oh, look, you worry too much! Darlin', I've got every intention of gettin' her into a home one day soon. *Don't* worry about that. But for the moment let's just give it a go. Let's get the place sold; see what we get for it. We'll take her out for a drive later and see if we can get her to be more social. It'll be fine, love. Trust me.'

Chapter 6

In the conservatory, Gloria sat sipping her tea, staring at their wonderful garden, abloom with blue agapanthus, white lace-cap hydrangeas and Nelly Moser clematis, which Val had carefully sown and nurtured over the years, wistfully draping itself along the bottom wall. To give Val her due, she was a very caring sort of person and perfectly suited to being a nurse. But Clegg, even though he was her son and she loved him dearly, Clegg was a bully. She'd always known it. Forgiven it but known it.

Oh, Arthur had always called Clegg a 'wild card'. He'd sailed too close to the wind in all manner of ways as a teenager and even managed to secure a few nights 'in clink' after one particular bloody episode of fighting, when he'd yelled at the arresting officer that he wished him dead in a very gruesome sort of way . . .

It had piqued Gloria, back then, that her son always dealt with all his problems via his fists. They certainly hadn't brought him up to be like that. Arthur, usually affably patient, had finally snapped and told him to go get signed up and do his bit. Well, he'd got no other prospects when he left school and fighting with other kids on the estate seemed to be the common order of the day – *every* time he went out. In fact, he seemed to be a very angry young man, most of the time, and nobody knew why. Least of all Cleggy. So Arthur hoped the army might channel his energies in a more positive way.

'You know, half me troubles are because of me name, Dad! Who in their right mind would give me the name of some stupid old fogey on *Last of the Summer Wine*? Ain't gonna put me right in me mates' eyes, is it, Dad?'

But Arthur wasn't to blame. He'd loved all the old comedies, as had Gloria. They'd roared at the exploits of characters in the likes of *The Good Life*, *Steptoe and Son*, *Only Fools and Horses* and the rest. Those were the days of endless good telly and irascible characters. In fact, Arthur had taken *pride* in the fact he'd given his son the name of a lovable household character, who'd caused millions of people to roll about laughing at the foibles of life.

'But you've got a mate called Baron. What the 'eck is that about, son? Least Clegg is unique.'

'It's unique, Dad, 'cos no one else friggin' wants a stupid name like that!'

Gloria had thought that, perhaps, Clegg's name hadn't helped matters. But, finally, after all her son's troubles and a succession of failed relationships, he met a much older yet volatile woman called Babs who'd entered his life with three kids and a shed-load of her own problems; including a jealous ex-husband who'd sent Clegg flying through the doors of A&E

and yet – fortunately – straight into the caring arms of nurse Valerie Robson.

Luckily Val had been his perfect foil and straightened him out, as far as Gloria could tell. He'd met her late in the day, as it were, but they'd still gone on to have the football-mad Adam and little sister Jessie, her perfect grandchildren.

Gloria often found herself thinking about the fun they'd had when Clegg and Val visited with the children when Arthur was alive. Those days were a mixed bag of memories but mainly sweet ones, Gloria chose to believe.

Well, she'd had nothing else to think about whilst being cooped up in her son's house for these past two weeks with only the TV for company. They wouldn't let her do anything or help out around the house, not even laying or clearing the table for breakfast or dinner. They just kept telling her to sit down and relax or watch TV. Yet since being deposited here with Clegg and Val, Gloria noted that her grandchildren were nowhere to be seen. She'd adored little Jessie and Adam but they hadn't been brought to visit her in *ages*. She was trying to remember their last visit – gosh, probably a good ten or eleven years ago. The last time was when Jessie tripped and fell over some of the clutter in the lounge. My goodness, how she howled! So she'd've been around seven. They'd both be teenagers now.

Clegg explained that they weren't currently at home because it was the school holidays so they were off camping in Wales with a load of their school chums and *should* be back home next week. Gloria couldn't understand his emphasis on the word 'should'. *Were they coming back or weren't they?* What was that all about? Or had they turned into uncontrollable tearaways, since she'd last seen them? If they were in their teens now it could be a troubling time for them, Gloria thought, recalling her own problems with Clegg at that age. *His* problems had brought other boys' mothers to their door, complaining about her son's aggression. Or the school always phoning and wanting to see her. Once they'd even had a brick thrown through their window. Very unsettling times, they were.

However, the children's holiday week had come and gone but there was still no sighting of Jessie and Adam. Gloria crept upstairs into their bedrooms, when Clegg and Val were at work, and looked at their things. There were lots of photos on their walls but Gloria didn't recognise anyone in them.

Yet, as Gloria sipped her tea in the conservatory, something felt amiss. She didn't know what it was but there was a lot of whispering going on and she didn't like that. It made her feel awkward, as though she shouldn't really be there. Perhaps Clegg and Val weren't getting on any more. She hadn't seen them together in a long time. Who knows what goes on in families, she thought. Or perhaps it was something else entirely.

In the past, when Clegg visited, he'd always come by himself, apart from once, when Val accompanied him. On that particular day she'd walked round moaning about every aspect of Gloria's home, especially her collections of things, and she'd wanted to start chucking it all out onto the streets, for heaven's sake! Gloria soon put a stop to that, with some choice words. Perhaps that's why she'd never been round since.

'Oh, Val's workin', Mum. She's always workin'. It's a callin' being a nurse, folk say,' he'd usually explain, by way of an apology.

That aside, it also upset Gloria that Clegg had never even thought to take her back to *their* house for a cuppa or a meal, which would've been just wonderful for a change. Plus she'd've got to see the children more.

So even though she was staying with them, whilst she knew her house was being sorted out and even though everything was very nice, in an odd contrived sort of way – well, the central heating and hot water, especially, were very nice – she just didn't feel comfortable with this arrangement. She felt out of place. It was as though she was somewhere she wasn't meant to be. Plus she didn't know how to respond or talk to Val yet. She wasn't even sure they had anything in common any more.

She couldn't wait to get back to her own home, once it was sorted out. That was a comforting thought at least.

Val's beautiful garden seemed to stare at Gloria as she sat lost in thought but Gloria Frensham wasn't really looking at any of it.

Chapter 7

'Jocelyn, it's Gloria!'

Jocelyn was taken aback. Well, she'd never expected a call from her arch-rival. In fact, she'd never had the time of day for the woman who'd been a thorn in her side, one way or another, over all these years because of Tilsbury. Not that he was a real catch by any means. Ha, their rows had been famous over the years. But there had been a time when they'd gotten on a treat.

'What the effin' hell do you want?'

'And it's great to talk to you too, ducks! Look, can't we put all that stuff behind us, now? It's been going on for years! We were lovely friends once –'

'Yeah but nicking someone else's husband ain't playin' fair, Glor!'

'Oh rubbish, Joss! You kicked him out! And he hadn't done nothing wrong. He likes animals! You got it all wrong and he used that as a reason to leave, is all. How many times do we have to go over old ground? Plus he came to me. Not the other way round. I was happy with my Arthur.'

Gloria paused, wondering if Jocelyn was still listening.

'Besides you're tied up with Marvin now. And he treats you right, by all accounts. Can't have 'em both, lovey. Anyway, I'm ringing to ask a favour. I expect you know what's gone on, ducks. And we both know Clegg's a bit of a twat when it comes to Tilsbury. But he looks after me, he does. They both do, in their way. But, that aside, I need to talk to Tils. Want to apologise to him about all this. Don't mind if you want to pass the message on. Or else I can speak to him, if you give him this number and get him to ring. But it'll have to be before six p.m., this week, cause Cleggy and Val are both workin' 'til then and I don't want no trouble from them.'

Silence continued at the end of the line. Gloria didn't push it.

'I suppose!' Jocelyn said with a sigh.

'What do you suppose, ducks?'

'I'll tell him. But here, Glor. I'll tell you summat . . .'

'What Jocelyn?'

'Well, Tils was like, full of it, when your Cleggy chucked him out. I mean he says Cleggy literally got hold of him by the scruff of his collar and marched him down the stairs and out the door. Like, over all them things you have, and Cleggy was kicking stuff outta the way and stuff was breaking. Tinklies. You know? And then straight outta your house. Anyway, the next week there was a right racket, I can tell you –'

'Racket?'

'Oh yeah,' Jocelyn continued, excitedly. 'I went to see what

40

was going on, like, with Big Doreen from next door. And it was right astoundin' it was. Big lorries arrived and people with weird-looking gear on and masks over their faces. And they kept going in and out, and gettin' stuff and dumpin' it in the lorries. Just chuckin' it in, like. Stuff was crackin' and breakin'. And people were gawping at what was goin' on. You'd've be in the nursin' home by then. And after that the electricity people went in, to fix up your Big Bang. Then there were decorators and floorin' people. Gawd! It looked like a ruddy crime scene, it did, with all the vans and people swarmin' all around!'

'Crikey, Joss. That sounds like a whole load of crumblies!'

'Yeah, it was, Glor. But, you know, if you saw your place now you wouldn't recognise it. All your stuff's gone. To the dump, Tils says. He says it's all painted up, now: white walls and you've got a new kitchen and new bathroom. He snuck in and saw it after it was all done up. Plus there's three For Sale boards outside. They're sellin' it, Glor. Looks like Cleggy's sellin' your house from under ya, love.'

'He's what? No, he can't be! Don't be silly. He's meant to be sorting it all out for me. Not sellin' it, love! He didn't tell me he was sellin' it, Joss,' Gloria said, suddenly feeling sick. That *couldn't* be what was happening, surely. 'Crikey, ducks, are you sure?'

'So why else would there be sale boards outside it, then?'

'Definitely outside my place?' Gloria gasped. 'Not next door?'

'I seen 'em with my own eyes, Glor!'

She'd been told they were looking for the electrical fault. She'd never been told that Clegg wanted to do anything else. He told her he was going to put things right and she'd thought that meant that, once things had been sorted out, she'd just move back in and things would continue as normal. But, if what Jocelyn was saying was true then there'd be nothing left to go home for because ALL her stuff had apparently gone. To the DUMP. And new stuff was replacing her old things.

So maybe *that's* what was going on. Her son, Clegg, was trying to sell her house, on the quiet! Gloria felt weak with worry. *Oh my God!*

No, it couldn't be. Jocelyn must've got it wrong! Why would Clegg do something like that, without telling her? Why would he think it was *okay* to do something like that without telling her? Or did he just want her to live with them? They hadn't discussed anything like that. And no! Gloria didn't want to live with them – even though they were the only family she had now. She'd dreamt about it in the early days after Arthur died, of course, but it wasn't something she'd contemplated for a long time now. She'd grown to like living by herself. Plus there'd be rules at Clegg's and Tilsbury wouldn't be allowed to visit, for one thing.

Or else – no! *Surely not!*

A chill ran through Gloria. *Surely he didn't want to put her back into Green's Nursing Home, did he?* Or did he want to put her somewhere else, out of the way, so she'd be no trouble to anyone? Away from the people she loved and cared about . . . ?

What if that was his plan? They'd never really got on, mother and son, had they? Not really. It'd been much better and easier when Arthur was alive. Clegg had respected Arthur. But since then . . .

Or maybe that *was* his plan? To put her in an old people's home – sitting there, alongside moaning old folk, just like in that *Waiting for God* programme, and visited *even less* by her family. They had busy lives; Clegg was always telling her that. And then, eventually, she'd be *forgotten* . . .

No, Clegg! Surely *not that*!

How she used to laugh at that show! But it didn't seem quite so funny now she might end up in that same situation.

Realisation suddenly dawned that she was nearly eighty. She would eventually become a bind to her son and his family, so it would *definitely* be something they'd be discussing with her in the not-too-distant future, of that she was sure. It also hit her that they might be contemplating *where* to put her at this very moment in time, especially with this new problem of her house. Gloria knew she didn't feel ready for that kind of conversation. She was still able-bodied and, as far as she knew, she wasn't starting to lose her marbles just yet. And even though she could see she was seventy-nine on the outside, she certainly didn't feel like an old woman on the inside.

'You okay, Glor?' asked Jocelyn in a small, worried voice.

No, Gloria Frensham was not okay. A tear dripped slowly

down her cheek. She thanked Jocelyn, with a watery, 'Yeah but I, I gotta go now. So ta-ra, love. We'll speak soon.' And she put the phone down.

She simply couldn't believe what Jocelyn was suggesting, but Jocelyn wasn't prone to lying. Yet it really didn't seem feasible that Clegg would go behind her back and sell her property or get rid of all her belongings, without her knowledge. *Would he?* Did he really care *so little* for her feelings? Her mind was buzzing with all the questions, flying around inside her brain.

She desperately hoped that Jocelyn had got it completely wrong.

Chapter 8

Gloria slumped onto the stool by the phone in Clegg's hall, dumbfounded, trying to make sense of Jocelyn's news. She wiped her tears away, on the back of her sleeve.

She had to think this through.

She didn't want to jump to the wrong conclusion about her son. Relations between them were strained at best and, anyway, she had to live with him and his wife for the moment. But the more she thought about it she realised that no one had actually mentioned anything to her about her either returning to her own home, after the electrics had been fixed, or staying with them on a more permanent basis. They hadn't had any meaningful conversations with her about anything relating to her future. Or were things still being decided between them. Maybe that's what all the pussyfooting around was about?

Right, well, she had to get to grips with this. She had to get things clear in her own mind. She had to look at the facts. Fact One, she thought, taking a deep breath.

Her ruddy, difficult and annoying yet occasionally affable son; the son Arthur and she had tried to guide and love, despite his failings, had now, supposedly, in some wild turn of events decided to get rid of *everything* she'd ever owned. What? Even her jewellery? And what about all her precious photo albums? Some of her most valuable possessions were what she could see in those albums.

And there was lots of other stuff she really wanted to hold on to. There was Cleggy's little red three-wheeler tricycle that she'd kept, for starters, and the old Singer sewing machine for stitching Arthur's work shirts. Oh yes and then there was Cleggy's little finger paintings he did when he was at school and all those Plasticine models he made. And there was Arthur's collection of World War I planes and oh, there were lots of things she wanted to keep. Memories were attached to all of them. And memories were all she had left now. No! He couldn't have! He wouldn't have done all that, surely?

Would he?

Fact Two . . .

Jocelyn had said that Clegg had cleared everything else away too. Everything clogging up the rooms. All the crap, as Clegg always called it. Taken away in lorries! Well yes. If Gloria was honest she'd known that, one day, at some point, everything would have to be sorted out and most of it dumped; there'd been a vast amount of rubbish. Even Green's Nursing Home had given her some new clothes. They'd realised the blouses and skirts they'd found in her wardrobes, once they'd cleared everything out, were damp and would be too small for her now. The dresses Green's had given her, however, didn't fit her very well so she wanted to get some new ones when Val could take her.

Probably donated by families of people who died, Gloria thought, jokingly, and then stopped, realising that – oh my God – that could actually have been the truth.

Nonetheless, even though Gloria knew Clegg could be bloody-minded, she didn't really believe he'd get rid of all her personal belongings and knick-knacks, without telling her about it first. Or perhaps he didn't realise how important all that stuff was to her? It had been part and parcel of her and Arthur's life together. So surely he wouldn't be that inconsiderate, would he?

Fact Three . . .

By all accounts, Clegg had even got rid of dear Tilsbury, *and* told him never to come back! Well, how ridiculous! As if Tilsbury would do what her bully of a son told him. But to top it all off she'd also been told that Clegg was getting rid of her *house* as well now!

Gloria let out a deep sigh. The facts were alarmingly clear. It didn't look good, whatever Clegg was doing. Plus he'd discussed *none* of it with her beforehand.

So Jocelyn's news had been totally shattering – to the extent that Gloria didn't want to believe it was true. But Gloria had lived with her son long enough to realise that Cleggy was a force to be reckoned with. She knew *that* much, as his mother. And so, consequently, the facts seemed to stack up against him. Therefore, it was highly probable that Jocelyn's take on the situation was correct.

Nonetheless, she could see, on the other hand, that she'd never really know what was going on unless she confronted Clegg and Val about her suspicions. And that was something she certainly didn't want to face or do, right now.

Oh dear.

Why were things starting to go horribly wrong for her? How had her life suddenly turned out like this?

Chapter 9

The next day a despondent Gloria paced her bedroom until Clegg and Val went to work. Then she picked up their hall telephone to speak to Tilsbury. Jocelyn had kept her promise and Tilsbury had briefly rung Gloria back yesterday afternoon.

'Here, Glor, ring me back tomorrow at Jocelyn's, when the coast's clear and we can have a proper talk,' he'd said.

But, today, the last thing she wanted was for either Clegg or Val to come home, unexpectedly, and catch her on the phone to Clegg's dreaded nemesis, Tilsbury. All hell would break loose if they did. Of that she was sure.

Gloria hesitated before dialling Jocelyn's number and took a deep breath.

It was such a shame it all had to be like this, tiptoeing around everybody's personalities, for fear of reprisals, she thought. Why was family life so darned complicated sometimes?

If Adam and Jessie had been home instead of on their extended holiday with their respective friends, everything would've been so much better. In fact, staying with her son would've been far more bearable if her grandchildren had been home, despite the recent bad news from Jocelyn. Gloria also despised the fact that Clegg and Val seemed to be walking on eggshells around her and always whispering. Too much whispering was going on.

She rang her friend's number and Tilsbury answered immediately. 'All right, my love?'

'Not really, Tils. I'd like to see ya, if you're free today. Just need an ear to bend really. Someone to talk to about all this. Can't take it all in, ducks. It's such a shock. But if you're coming round you'll need to be quick. What? Why yes, my love. Why, that would be absolutely lovely, Tilsbury! Yes, okay. I'd love to do that. But we'd have to be back before they get home. They've been getting back around six this week. Yes, six. Right, so I'll expect you in about half an hour then and do NOT be late!'

Oh, but what a wonderful idea! Tilsbury said he wanted to take her out for afternoon tea. Yes! It might be just the thing she needed right now: a little treat, in amongst all their problems. They hadn't done anything like that in years – in fact, since Arthur was alive. Tilsbury said he knew she was upset by everything that'd happened and by what Jocelyn'd told her yesterday and he simply wanted to cheer her up.

Gloria had tossed and turned, restlessly, the night before, worrying about what Clegg was planning to do next, regarding her living arrangements. She was still mystified as to why he'd never mentioned selling her house to her. Or maybe she hadn't been listening when he'd come to fetch her that day; there'd been a lot going on. But why did he suddenly want to sell her house now?

Maybe he'd found other problems with the building. Maybe something was wrong with the drains or there was structural damage? Or maybe they'd discovered it was in one of those sink hole areas? She'd heard about that sort of thing once.

As she stood in the hall, anxiously waiting for Tilsbury to come and pick her up she was relieved that, at least, the nursing home people had been lovely and understanding about her problems. During their heart-to-hearts the social worker, Kate, had helped her 'come to terms' with the deaths of Arthur and her parents – her real parents and Alice.

'That's what we think your hoarding was about, my lovely. Just a reaction to your grief. And keeping things of sentimental value is understandable, Gloria. But we think it overwhelmed you. Can you see that trying to find an electrical fault amongst all that stuff could have been the death of you? Or what if you'd fallen and couldn't get back up? So we do hope you're not going to try to bring lots of unnecessary things back into your life, again. We're going to try and help you with that, over the coming weeks, and your family have said they'll be there for you, helping you with that, too.'

It had all sounded so nice and comforting. She'd chatted to the people at Green's Nursing Home about lots of things she couldn't talk about with anyone else. It was reassuring. And it now seemed she wasn't as mad as some people – ahem, *Clegg* – had made out. She'd been starting to feel more positive about life, until yesterday, when Jocelyn crumpled her world.

Anyway, she knew she had to try and focus and forget about her woes for one day, if she was to have a lovely afternoon out with Tilsbury, unbeknown to Clegg. She would definitely need to talk to her son about these things, at some point, but she didn't feel strong enough to cope with it all now.

She'd struggled to get into the coat Green's Nursing Home had supplied her, along with a pair of fuddy shoes, and another ill-fitting Crimplene dress.

And that was another thing! Her daughter-in-law had promised they'd go shopping for new clothes when they got back from the nursing home. Unfortunately, all Val's good intentions hadn't materialised yet. And the only conversations she'd had with her was when Val insisted that Gloria should relax in the conservatory or watch the television, when they were out.

'You'll need to be patient with us, for a while, Gloria, because we're a very busy family at the moment,' Val explained, when Gloria first arrived.

Well, Gloria had sat obediently waiting for some attention from them, for weeks. But the days had crept by, which was okay at first because she could watch all the TV programmes she liked and there was food aplenty. But – apart from one afternoon's drive to a lovely public garden somewhere – Gloria hadn't left the house at all. Nor had she had a proper conversation with them about anything. The whole 'process' of being with them had simply felt awkward and contrived.

Anyway, not wanting to give her son any further reason for alarm or arguments, she wrote a short note, telling them she was going out for tea 'with a friend' so they wouldn't worry.

Ratta-tat went a knock on the door. Gloria pulled it open.

'Oh my God, Tilsbury! We're not going on that are we?'

Gloria, in her tight-fitting coat, slightly oversized shoes and pale pink polka dot dress that, ordinarily, she wouldn't be caught dead in, stared in astonishment at the scabby, clapped-out scooter she knew belonged to Jocelyn.

'It's okay, Glor. It goes at least. It'll get us into town, anyways. I got her helmet for you. The cops won't pull us over with helmets on!'

'But I'm wearing a ruddy DRESS, Tils, and I'm seventy-nine!'

Tilsbury tried to not laugh at the vision forming in his mind.

'Aw, c'mon, Glor! It don't matter what you got on. Live a little. You've been stuck in that ruddy overcrowded house since forever! C'mon, my love. This'll just be a one-off trip down memory lane. Like old times? Anyways, Jocelyn gave us a fiver to get tea in the park gardens.'

Gloria laughed heartily. 'Bloody nicked it you mean! Christ, Tils, you're the man! Okay, okay. Well, how to do this then? Least it's not far I suppose, is it?'

'No, Glor, and I'll go the back lanes. And I'll getcha back in time for your bloody rotten son!'

Gloria shook her head. It seemed like a crazy idea.

Ordinarily she wouldn't entertain such madness. A thought popped into her head – why didn't Jocelyn ever call the police over Tilsbury's nicking sprees? He had clearly nicked that fiver! She wondered if Jocelyn still had a soft spot for the irascible man, like everyone did. *Apart from Clegg.* Perhaps that was it. Perhaps that's why she lent him the scooter. Or did he steal that too?

Gloria sighed. What to do?

However, whilst studying her dress and handbag and knowing none of it was ideal to be riding a scooter in, she came to a snap decision. At least it was a warm sunny summer's day, with a slight mischievous breeze, ripe for fun.

Oh what the hell!

'Okay, Tilsbury. Shift forward and let me on. And hold it steady – and I mean steady. And if you start larkin' about on it, I'm gettin' off. Plus you'll have to help me get me leg over.'

Tilsbury couldn't stop himself chuckling at that.

'Oi! I meant over the *seat*, you bad man! Here! You got enough fuel in it? I don't want us breakin' down en route.'

Chapter 10

It had been a bumpy, ungainly ride to the tea rooms, that afternoon.

Tilsbury chuckled to himself every time Gloria let out a yelp when they went over a pothole or swerved to avoid something unsavoury in the road. She was sure he was driving scarily on purpose but clung on tight when he went round bends. She hoped they wouldn't see anyone they knew and was just starting to relax into his particular way of riding when they arrived.

Tilsbury stopped the engine and held the scooter steady whilst Gloria slipped forward and struggled to get off, straightening her dress and hooking her bag back over her arm. She muttered a little but otherwise acknowledged she had actually arrived safely.

The young girl at the counter in the Park Gardens Tea Room frowned when Tilsbury told her he didn't have enough to pay for two cream teas consisting of scrummy-looking fruit scones, jam, cream and tea for two.

The bill came to £5.90 but Tilsbury didn't have any more than the fiver Jocelyn had given him. And there was NO way he'd ask Gloria for the extra. This was supposed to be his treat to her. He hadn't taken her out in ages and it felt good doing something for her after all this time.

'Couldn't we do a deal here, love? Me an' the missus – well, we're quite poor, you see. Don't have much at our age apart from our meagre pensions. Don't even go out much, either, you know?'

The youngster was on her own whilst the other waitress was outside taking orders and clearing tables. Tilsbury had clocked that there didn't seem to be anyone else in charge, on the premises.

'Um well, okay. But what I could do is cut the scone in half, with the two teas and then – I'm not supposed to – but I could give you two biscuits as well. And then I can charge you for one tea and one cream tea for £4.05. Let's say £4.00. And you'll get the biscuits for free. Would that be all right?'

Tilsbury chuckled to himself. *Clever girl.* He'd still got a deal and some change to boot.

He nodded with a big grin. 'That'd be just fine, my love!'

He carried the laden tray over to Gloria sitting by the window. She'd deemed it a little too blowy to be sitting outside. But her eyes lit up as Tilsbury set the table with their cream tea.

'Cor, Tils. I haven't had a ruddy cream tea in absolutely years!'

'I know, my love. So get stuck into that one then. Bet you're glad you came out with me now, aren't you!'

Gloria nodded vigorously, chomping down on her half of the scone, caked with cream and strawberry jam.

'S'lovely!' Gloria murmured, as a few crumbs spilled onto her lap.

* * *

A cream tea amongst the colourful herbaceous perennials of the Park Garden Tea Rooms was completely delightful and both Gloria and Tilsbury sat patting their tums, afterwards, in appreciation.

Gloria reached out and got hold of Tilsbury's hand.

'That was crackin', Tils. And I do thank you from the bottom of me heart. You've always been a good 'un to me, ducks!'

'I've always had a soft spot for you, you know.'

Gloria wrinkled her nose. 'Oh, I know that, ducks, and I love ya to bits, too!'

'Right, well, Glor, we've still got some time before I takes ya back to yer miserable son. So, I'm thinking . . . How about – now wait for it! I remember you saying this to me, last year. How about a trip *to the seaside*? You said you hadn't been to the seaside since you were a girl!'

'*What?* We can't go there! We're miles away from the sea and I don't think that contraption outside will get me any further than back home, Tils.'

'Course it will, Glor. It got us here didn't it?'

'Yeah but that was only a couple of miles.'

'Now look, my love. When will we *ever* get to do summat like this again? This is a gas! I'm lovin' it and I don't want today to end. Do you? Besides the sea ain't that far away. An hour tops!'

Gloria looked out the window. Young families walked with children. A dog chased a frisbee. It was a pretty nice park as parks went.

Tilsbury sighed, despondently.

'But look, Gloria, what if Cleggy decides to put you in a nursing home, miles away from anywhere? We'd never get to see each other again. We'd never get to go to the sea or anywhere else. We'd never get to have any kind of fun ever again, Glor, would we? Remember those tea dances we all used to go to? That's all finished, now, my love. We – we're kinda near the end of those times now, aren't we, Glor?'

He reached out and stroked Gloria's scarred hands.

'Can't we – look! Can't we just have this one last wonderful day to remember for the rest of our lives? We're not gonna get another chance like this to create a new mem'ry now we're nearly in our eighties, are we, Glor?'

Gloria shrugged, thinking he was probably right. Life was over when you hit a certain age, she knew that much.

'And, you're right, me scooter probably won't last much longer but I truly believe it will get us to the beach . . . Just for that one last time, eh, Glor?'

Tilsbury noticed that tears were starting to form in Gloria's eyes.

'Oh Tils!' Gloria said, dabbing at her eyes with a serviette. 'You've got me thinkin' about things again, ducks. And, yes, we did have some crackin' times, didn't we? All of us together: you, me, Arthur and Jocelyn once upon. They were good times. You're right. But we're a couple of old fogies now. I ain't got the energy to be tearin' around all over the place. Look we'd best be off, now, Tils. I've truly had a lovely time, today, though. And it'll still be a wonderful mem'ry to look back on.'

Gloria slowly rose from her seat and struggled into her coat again with Tilsbury's help.

He looked so downbeat Gloria couldn't meet his gaze. But she was reliving the past, now he'd mentioned it. She was thinking about how their lives were, indeed, fluttering towards the bottom of the hill they'd once climbed so eagerly in their youth. She let out a sigh as they ambled down the steps of the café, arm in arm to steady themselves and across the freshly cut lawn to where Tilsbury had parked the scooter.

Gloria studied the etched, weather-beaten lines across Tilsbury's sunburnt face. She knew her seventy-nine-year-old face had its own share of lines both from worry, when Clegg was a boy getting into scrapes, and those joyous times when Clegg and Val had angelic babies of their own. She'd known some very happy as well as some very sad times.

But Tilsbury was right.

There really wasn't much else to look forward to, now, at their time of life. Gloria also realised that Clegg wouldn't want her to live with them for the rest of her life, either, whatever her hopes might once have been for that. And from what she'd learned recently, she was certain he'd make darned sure that an old people's home, somewhere, would soon start calling her name . . .

So she came to her second big decision of the day.

'Oh stuff it! Crumblies be gone! C'mon then, Tils. Start the motor. Let's see where this old heap'll take us one last time . . .'

Chapter 11

'Wheeeeeeeee –' Gloria shrieked as the little scooter sped along at an eye-watering forty miles per hour towards the azure sea, the wind batting her new hairstyle, that warm July morning. She'd misplaced Jocelyn's helmet at the gas station, when Tilsbury had filled up for the rest of their journey, so her eyes were, indeed, watering with all the wind and grit. But they'd grabbed some sandwiches, a couple of cans of fizzy pop and two cheap beach towels and she'd paid for the lot with the credit card – the one Cleggy had got for her, which she'd never actually used before.

'And this's on you, Miserable Son! Well, you give it to me for essentials and emergencies, so I vow that I will spend it on all the essentials we need – things for the beach – and any *emergencies* that might befall us, like making sure this crappy moped thingy gets us from A to Z. In other words, my dear Tils, we're gonna *enjoy* today!'

In fact, Gloria had happily decided to shut down her worries for today. Trepidation of all things unknown was no longer her concern and nor was getting back to Cleggy and Val before they got home. Whatever the rest of the day brought, so be it. There was no way Gloria was going to be dictated to by her son. *She* was the mother, after all, and so *she'd do* as she darn well pleased.

Oh yes! Gloria Frensham was enjoying this. She was actually *having fun.* Gloria Frensham couldn't remember the last time she'd had any *fun.* When you hit that mysterious age that some youngsters deem 'old' – and which could be any age over thirty (or even less) – you weren't supposed to be having fun, were you? You were supposed to be sitting down in a comfortable armchair, somewhere, sipping tea, watching TV reruns, and being perfectly respectable, calm and fuddy.

That, she could now see, was what Clegg and Val had been trying to make her do – conform to that ideal. '*Keeps 'em quiet!*' she'd actually heard a youngster in Green's Nursing Home say.

So today – and just for today – Gloria Frensham was reverting to her younger self, Miss Gloria Howe, attracting the likes of Tilsbury and his buddies, when he'd returned to Norwich with his family after years away in India.

Gloria and Jocelyn had hung round Ron's Transport Café, on the outskirts of town. Lorry drivers used to come in to fill up with fuel and have a bite to eat. It was also where the local motorbike riders used to stop off for the same reason, which, in turn, attracted young and reckless lasses from miles around. It was quite a hub and quickly became known as Babe Magnet Café. Gloria and Jocelyn were always there, even got Saturday waitressing jobs there for a while, after they left school and before they became secretaries. Those *were* the days.

After about an hour's drive and a detour due to roadworks, Tilsbury finally pulled into a small car park, leading down to a beach. There were only two other cars there, as well as an ice-cream van with a youngster inside, tapping away on his phone.

'Where the 'eck are we, Tils?' said Gloria, easing herself off the scooter and taking her coat off.

'Dunno, my love, that detour threw me a bit. But I can see the sea.'

Gloria stood, allowing the heat of the sun to kiss her skin. Ah, it felt wonderful. She closed her eyes and allowed the warmth to wash over her until Tilsbury got the stand down on the scooter. Then they linked arms and took their carrier bag of goodies and tentatively made their way down to the beach. It was quite a trek but they took it slowly. Gloria laid the beach towels on the soft beige and shingle sand when they finally arrived, a little out of breath.

'Plonk yer bum on that, Tils!'

But Tilsbury shook his head. 'Nah. I'm off for a spot of paddlin', Glor!' he said and promptly pulled off all his clothes.

'Good grief, Tils! Have you lost yer mind?' she gasped in awe, looking around in case anyone had seen what was going on. There were a few holidaymakers further down the long stretch of beach but no one nearby, thankfully.

She couldn't remember the last time she'd seen her old friend strip-Jack naked.

'Well why not, Glor?' he retorted, as he picked his way down to the edge of the sea.

'Oi but it's bloody *freezin'*, Glor!' he yelled back.

'You havin' a swim, then?' Gloria shouted to him. 'When was the last time you swam, Tils?'

'Who cares, my love. You comin' in for a paddle? You can't come all this way and not come in for a paddle!'

Gloria shook her head fiercely and said, more to herself than Tilsbury, 'No way! You're mad!'

But she could see that all their talk of days gone by meant Tilsbury was lost to the frivolity of his youth.

What *on earth* were they doing?

Gloria Frensham also realised she was not herself. She was a shade of the person she'd been a few hours ago. And now that new woman was stumbling down to the edge of the sea, discarding her shoes, stockings and dress, as she picked her way over the shingle in her full-length underskirt and waded into the freezing water beside her old friend. And he – in turn – recognised Gloria Howe: a sexy little beastie from way back in the day!

She introduced her aged body bit by bit, step by step to the chilly sea and squealed when the water reached her middle. Pah! But she'd known far worse in her life. So, gritting her teeth, she dropped straight into the cold water and then swam along near the beach a few strokes, her teeth chattering.

What would Clegg think if he could see them both now?

Tilsbury waded towards her and then allowed himself to submerge, jumped up again – shivering – then he too swam along beside her for a while.

'Can't feel my ruddy fingers, Tils. I'll have to get out, now.'

'Yeah. I'm freezin' me ruddy balls off too!' he yelled.

And they laughed like they'd not laughed in a long while, both staggering to help each other out of the freezing sea and back to where they'd left their clothes, strewn all over the beach.

* * *

Between them they helped each other dry off. Tilsbury held the towel around Gloria's body whilst she struggled back into her polka dot dress.

'Oh yuk. And it's all itchy and horrible. We need comfort at our age, don't we, Tils?'

'It's the salt water, love. Here, let me rub it a bit more with my towel. It's drier than yours.'

'We must be mad, Tils. What the 'eck would everyone think of us if they saw us now?'

'Bloody stuff 'em, Glor. Who gives one! This is our adventure, anyways.'

The young man serving at the ice-cream van gave them a brisk smile as they ambled up to his window with wet hair, purple lips and panting from the walk back up from the beach.

'I see you've been enjoyin' yerselves out there! Aren't you cold?'

Tilsbury nodded. 'Course we're cold, son. We're bloody pensioners. Bloody freezin' out there. But we've made it back to the land of the livin' and now we're wantin' a hot cuppa or three. Do you do tea?'

Tilsbury and Gloria sat on a nearby bench, gratefully sipping their hot tea and eating their sandwiches as they watched a gang of young people arrive, whooping and hollering and running off down the beach. They could hear them larking around and squealing and probably splashing each other like they used to do when they were kids.

'Well, the Maldives it ain't, Glor, but have you enjoyed today?'

Gloria was a changed woman. Sure, she was still a bit shivery, damp and itchy and her nice new hairstyle was wet. She'd chucked her underskirt and stockings away because there was no way of drying them, and her coat was a bit creased from it being crumpled on the sand. But she was ecstatically happy. Her whole body felt alive and buzzy. She felt younger and more vibrant than she had in years.

'Oh yes, ducks,' she said, gathering up the empty sandwich packets and wondering what to do with them. 'I've had an amazing time today and I don't want to go home!'

She could see there was a bin next to the ice-cream van, so that's where she knew the rubbish needed to go. But putting rubbish in an actual bin was an unfamiliar experience for Gloria.

She hesitated and glanced at Tilsbury. As she looked at him, she felt as if she was alive with vitality.

He nodded. 'I believe you, my love. And we don't have to go home yet, if you don't want to. But I don't know where we can go to next. Do you? Or should we just take our time getting back?'

Gloria's shoulders fell and her demeanour changed.

She looked up as one of the youngsters came running back up, out of breath, and bought six cans of Coke and some chocolates for his friends. Gloria left the bench and slowly walked towards the bin. She couldn't take the rubbish with her on the scooter so it would have to go in the bin. But she hesitated again.

'Crazy isn't it, Tils. We're a couple of old farts, shivering on a beach, when we could be tucked up in a nice old people's home, somewhere, eatin' jelly and ice cream.'

'True. But where would you rather be?'

Gloria shrugged. 'Yes well, I've had an absolute ball, ducks. But I'm getting cold now so I suppose we ought to get back to reality.'

'Reality, Glor? Who's to say that this ain't reality? We're here on a day out. That's our reality for the moment. We're not doin' anything wrong. We're just two friends having a lovely day out. And it's not a dream. This is real.'

'Uh-huh. But people will start worryin' about us and then there'll be trouble. And I bet Cleggy will go mad when he knows I've come away with you.'

'You didn't tell him we were going out for the day, did you?'

'Of course not but I left a note saying I was going out with a friend and they know I don't have any friends to speak of. They'll work it out, Tils. I just got you and Jocelyn and my only other friend, Mabel, who lives with her family near Skegness –'

Gloria stopped, looked down at her sandy feet and then back up at Tilsbury. She'd not seen hide nor hair of Mabel since she'd upped sticks with Gerard and her kids and left for a better life in the Lincolnshire Fens, after he'd lost his job in Norwich in the Eighties. Oh sure, she'd had plenty of postcards and letters raving about the 'beach life' and entertainment along the proms in the summer and, yes, a few photos of the kids growing up. But it wasn't the same, communicating by post or the occasional phone call, was it? Not really. And not when they used to be so close.

A huge grin filled Gloria's cheeks, as she suddenly lifted the top of the bin and pushed the sandwich packets in.

'Oh stuff it! I want to go and see my friend Mabel in Skeggy, Tils. She's been sending me postcards for years but I've never been to Skeggy. She says the air there is fresh and bracing!'

Chapter 12

'Holy shit!'

As Tilsbury looked down at their squashed scooter, he knew Gloria's dreams were over. Not that he'd had any intention of attempting to take her to Skegness on the back of that ropey thing. It might've got them home. It would never have made it down major roads, into another county. But they wouldn't be leaving the beach the same way they'd arrived, that was for sure. And it'd be a helluva walk back to Norwich.

'Oh, Glor, I'm so sorry. Well, that's it, old girl. Game, set and match, as they say.'

He bent down to try and twist the handlebars back to their usual position. They were set at a funny angle. The front wheel was twisted too. Possibly it had fallen over and then a car backed over it when they were swimming. Or was it those pesky youngsters?

Tilsbury said he'd sort things out and moved off to talk to the boy in the ice-cream van. There was nothing to indicate that a bus stopped there regularly. So they'd need to get a lift. Or hitch. But Gloria wasn't sure anyone would stop for an elderly couple.

Mikey, the youngster serving ice creams to a family who'd just arrived, confirmed there were no buses but said he could give them a lift to Sheringham, where he lived, after he finished up. It wasn't busy enough for him to stay much longer, he told them.

'Might be a bit of a squash in this old rig amongst the fridges. Ha, ha. But at least it'll get you to civilisation.'

'Gee thanks, Mikey.'

Result! And yes it was a bit of a squeeze because he had to move the boxes of cornets and chocolate flakes to accommodate them and it was an uncomfortable ride, the two of them squashed in the back, like that. But after fifteen minutes or so Mikey pulled up and dropped them off by a seafront hotel so they could use the phone or whatever.

They waved goodbye to him and went inside the hotel.

'Well I dunno about you, Tils, but I'm bushed. I've not had this much fun or exercise in years! So I think I'm going to stay here the night, if I can. I just do not want the fuss I'm gonna get from my son, later on. I do not need his nonsense today. This is my adventure. And then I can go home – if you can call it that – tomorrow.'

'Wow! So despite all the panicking about Cleggy, you're really gonna stay here the night? Now that's what I'd call adventureful! You gonna ring them first?'

Gloria shrugged. 'Can't be arsed really, to be truthful. But I need a bath and a cuppa and then I'll think about it. What do you wanna do about things? D'you wanna stay too?'

Tilsbury shrugged as well. This was not how he thought the day was going to turn out.

He wasn't averse to life throwing curve balls. It'd been doing it to him all his life. But he had nowhere he could call home, to go back to. Perhaps it was time he stopped all his dossing around and to-ing and fro-ing and found himself permanent lifetime digs. Gloria was right. They should be thinking about where they ought to spend their twilight years. They were old folks, for God's sake, not kids, running around like they used to. Old age had suddenly arrived. Aches and pains would soon start setting in.

Plus Gloria's house was about to be sold, so she'd lost her forever home now. And he'd lost another occasional bed for the night. He'd been thinking for a while that he ought to talk to social services about getting some full-time accommodation when he got back and then sort his life out once and for all.

'Okay, well, yes! Do you mind if I stay too? P'raps Marvin'll come get me tomorrow. And I'll pay you back when I can, Glor.'

'No, Tils. This is going to be my treat. Well, actually it's going to be Cleggy's treat because I intend to use his credit card again. More essential purchases, of course! Stuff Cleggy! I don't like his attitude towards you. And I don't like his attitude, these days, full stop. So this is his penance!'

'Oo-er! Well, only if you're sure, Gloria. I don't want you gettin' into any trouble because of this!'

71

'I've no intention of gettin' into any trouble over this either, Tils! Things feel different for me now and life's gone a bit barmy and not in a bad way, I might add. I'm startin' to have some wonderful adventures and all that takes a bit of gettin' used to. But Cleggy's making matters much worse than they need to be.'

Tilsbury patted Gloria's hand, and smiled. 'Well okay, then. As long as you're sure!'

'I'm sure, Tils. Right! Well, I'm going to see if we can get booked in. And it'll be *twin* beds if there's no singles before you go gettin' ideas, ducks. And I bags the bathroom first.'

'Oh I won't be wantin' a bath, Glor. You know me. Can't be bothered with all that!'

'Ha! Under normal circumstances it wouldn't worry me what you do, Tils, but you're a bit stinky and if you're stayin' with me in the same room you're certainly gonna be havin' a bath *and* washin' yer hair, even if I have to throw you in myself!'

* * *

What a joy it was, waking up to the sound of the sea swishing along the beach, gulls screeching, and laughing holidaymakers starting to enjoy their day! They had a partial view of the sea from their bedroom window. Gloria stood for a moment, wrapped in a clean white towel, after her second bath in sixteen hours, peering out at the sight that befell her.

'Ah, will you look at that, Tils. Look! There's a big boat on the horizon. Makes me feel like a ruddy teenager again, like when we used to go to Yarmouth. I'm so happy.'

It was also a wonderful treat, later, to be eating the sumptuous fry-up of eggs, bacon, sausage, fried tomato and diced potatoes for breakfast, with lashings of tea and toast.

'I feel like a ruddy king, Glor. Don't think I've ever stayed in a hotel by the sea before. Tryin' to think where me and Jocelyn used to go.'

'Think you went caravanning a couple of times before you split up, didn't you? Somewhere near Hunstanton, wasn't it? You ever been abroad?' Gloria said, her mouth full of egg and toast.

Tilsbury slurped his tea. 'No, my love. You?'

'Just to Benidorm with Arthur for that overdue honeymoon. Well, we'd got those passports, you know. Bit of a just-in-case event. So we used 'em. Wasn't really Arthur's scene. But we had a full week of glorious sunshine and lots of cheap red wine. Never been anywhere else though. Took Cleggy to Bournemouth once but the rest of the time, you know, just the usual. Around here really.'

Tilsbury put his knife and fork together and sighed and stretched. 'Well that was lovely, Glor. So what do we do now? Shall we take a stroll? Take in the sea air before we surrender our lives to the crap we have to put up with back home?'

Gloria nodded, surprising him. 'There's no rush, is there?

We'll be back there soon enough. But I must say I've really, completely enjoyed this wonderful trip away. And thanks for starting the ball rolling by arranging that lovely afternoon tea for me, ducks. I'll never forget these last twenty-four hours.'

Chapter 13

Gloria and Tilsbury walked along the seafront, arm in arm, noticing the little waves slapping the beach and kiddies paddling or patting buckets of sandcastles. A young couple strolled past with huge dripping ice creams. It was another lovely sunny day with a light breeze rolling in off the sea. Gloria breathed in the salty sea air.

'Actually, Tils, I think I might just go into the actual town and get myself some new clothes, while I'm here. There's nothing at Val's apart from another weird dress Green's Nursin' Home gave me. Well something needs doing and Val says she's not had time to sort things out for me. She's got a demanding job as we all know. So I might as well. Do you want to come with me or do you want to ring Joss or Marv now?'

Tilsbury shrugged. 'Whatever, my love. But it's so nice here I think I'd quite like havin' a mooch around the shops, with you, Glor. Only been here once before – no I tell a lie. I came once with Marvin for a job interview, back in the day. And I came that other time with the lads for a boozy day out after I gave up work on account of me injury. D'you remember? Got into trouble for fightin' after old Jonesy bumped into that guy at the bar. Weren't his fault but all hell broke loose!'

'Uh-huh. Didn't you all end up in clink for the night?'

'We did, my love. It was an experience and a half that was!' Tilsbury chuckled.

Gloria couldn't remember the last time she'd been shopping with anyone. Living in her house under the strain of her hoarding problems had made her think she was incapable of living what she believed to be a normal life. She'd even considered herself old, past it and, yes, ready for the nearest old people's home. But actually, she realised, she wasn't any of those things. Her previous circumstances had seemed impossible to break out of. But the kind nursing home staff had opened her eyes and, now, she had no intention of closing herself down like that, ever again.

So she and Tilsbury went shopping. Tilsbury was happy enough to sit, whistling, outside the shops whilst she went in and bought three new dresses, underwear, a nice new jacket, a couple of scarves and a new pair of shoes that were comfy to walk in. She even bought a tiny, lightweight suitcase to put them all in; all her new possessions.

'There! I feel like I'm properly on my holidays now!' Gloria grinned. 'And these,' she said handing Tilsbury a plastic bag with a trouser leg hanging out, 'are for you!'

He jumped in surprise. 'W-what do you mean, Glor?'

'Well they're not actually new clothes, Tils. I got them from that charity shop over there. Clegg would kill me if he saw

I'd been buyin' you clothes on his credit card but he'll never know what I bought in there. No, don't try to argue. I know what you wear is the extent of your wardrobe and I'm not tryin' to control you or anything. I've only bought you one new change of clothes, like you had before. You're about the size of my Arthur before he put all that weight on. So I hope they fit. But you are very stinky, Tils. I never really noticed it before when we were in my house. But people keep staring at you.'

Tilsbury opened his mouth to speak but nothing came out.

'So we'll go back to the hotel now and try all this lot on properly, have a cuppa, check out and then ring people. Okay?'

Tilsbury nodded, dumbly.

No one had bought him clothes of any kind before. It was a sweet thing for her to do. But he could see Gloria was on a mission, with a new-found confidence to boot and so, no, he had no intention of arguing with her.

* * *

Their new purchases fitted a treat but Tilsbury's new jumper was a teeny bit big on him. He said he loved it anyway and put it round his shoulders. So Gloria bundled all their old stuff into the plastic bags. She could see it wouldn't all fit in the tiny room bin and wondered if she could find a new purpose for it back home.

Ah, but she'd promised Green's Nursing Home she wouldn't

keep stuff any more! Yes, that's what she'd actually agreed with them. So what to do? Hmm. Well, perhaps she could just leave it *by* the bin? Then maybe someone else could decide what to do with all the bags? Yes, that's what she'd do.

So Gloria carefully arranged the plastic bags full of old clothes around the bin in the bedroom. She could see she was starting to get used to the idea of getting rid of things she didn't need now. It's what other people did all the time and she was chuffed she was doing it herself, now, too.

She walked downstairs to reception, refusing to worry about the old clothes any more and paid for their stay. Then they went into the bar and ordered tea.

'Do you mind if I have a small lager, though, Glor?'

She acquiesced.

This mini holiday was a one-off anyway and she already knew Tilsbury's old problems with alcohol meant that, even now, he still sometimes fought with drinking the way she'd fought against people calling her a hoarder over the years. They were neither of them perfect and that sat okay with her.

'So that'll be two small lagers instead of the tea,' she said to the barman, with a wink.

Chapter 14

After discussing with Tilsbury how they were going to get home, he said he'd sort it and went to speak to the barman. When he returned he told Gloria that he'd rung Jocelyn and she'd promised to come and fetch them both. But she'd only come and fetch them *providing* someone was prepared to treat her to lunch, due to the 'accident' with her scooter and helmet, even though she hadn't used either of them in years.

Gloria chuckled and said she would be happy to buy Jocelyn lunch and Tilsbury said he owed both ladies 'big time'.

They had fish and chips in a little café off the High Street.

'Cor, it's marvellous this is, Glor. Haven't been treated to a meal out in a long time,' said Jocelyn, with a mouthful of chips. 'Plus it's nice to get away for a while, but I'm makin' apologies for my little clapped-out Mini before we leave 'cos it ain't as fit as it used to be. Not much room in it either.'

'Well thanks for offering me a lift, too, Joss. Didn't want to ring Val or Clegg and get an earful 'cos I *know* that's what I'll get eventually. Families, eh?'

Jocelyn nodded solemnly, pushing her mopped-up plate to

one side. 'Gotta tell you this, though, Glor. Bumped into that Mrs Daly at the shops. She's Clegg's neighbour and couldn't wait to tell me Clegg was heard yelling last night when you dint come back. He rang me, you know – Cleggy – and asked where Tilsbury was!'

'I left him a ruddy note, I did.'

'Yeah but there was no time on it and you didn't say *who* you'd gone off with. S'pose it had them worried. Anyway, Val was heard shouting back that she'd got enough on her plate, what with work.'

'Yeah, semi-detached walls can be a bit thin. And that Daly woman is a nosy old stick. Oh well. I'll ring 'em before we leave and tell 'em I'm on my way back.'

Yes, Gloria knew her mini holiday was definitely over. And reality – she was sure – was going to be a very LARGE flea in her ear, later that day!

As soon as she picked up the phone to speak to her son, she could tell Clegg was *raging*.

'Did you think it'd be helpful to not let us know your full intentions, Mother? They only just let you out of Green's. They could've kept you in longer and they would've done if we'd've thought you might be a danger to yourself. Val is furious. It's like you're taking the piss or laughing at us –'

'I'm not laughing at –'

'Or do we need to keep you under lock and key for your own good? Eh? Answer me that one.'

'I'm not a –'

'Well, I think it's high time you thought long and hard about the worry you've just put us through –'

'But I haven't –'

'And let me tell you if ANYTHIN' like this ever happens again, you'll be out of our house and into the nearest old people's home, quick march. There's no bloody point us giving you a roof over your head if you're going to throw it back in our face. DO YOU –'

'But I won't –'

'– UNDERSTAND?'

There was a tense pause.

Gloria knew anything else she might try and say would be pointless. Clegg would refuse to hear her. He always tried to talk over her, as if her opinion didn't matter. He simply treated her as if she were a silly little girl. And Gloria had no idea why he'd been treating her like this, since Arthur died. It was quite upsetting. She always felt as though she had to justify everything she did to him. *She* was supposed to be the mother, for God's sake!

So she dropped the receiver into the cradle and cut Clegg off with a click, without answering him.

A tear pricked her eye.

Well!

There was no way she could go 'home' now.

Chapter 15

Jocelyn dropped Gloria off at the station for her mid-afternoon train to Skegness. The hotel in Sheringham had kindly booked it for her. She'd have to make one change but she would simply ask someone at the train station how to do that. She'd loved being taken on trains, by her adopted mum, as a girl. She loved seeing all those possibilities of different places to live in, as well as those meandering rivers and quaint towns, whizzing past in the blink of an eye that she'd never get to visit.

She was set to wave a vigorous goodbye to Jocelyn and Tilsbury but then tottered back to their car, put her tiny case down and reached in to hug and kiss them both on the cheek, through the car windows, much to their surprise.

'We've been friends since forever, ducks, despite a few ups and downs but I still love youse both.'

Then she turned and ambled away before either of them noticed the tears trickling down her face. She didn't really know what she was doing or what she had to prove and whether it was to herself or everyone else. But there was no way she was returning to Clegg and Val at this moment in time. She was going to take some much-needed time out to think about things. And Mabel would know what she needed to do.

She'd recovered by the time she came to ask which platform she should be on for the first leg of her journey and settled down to read a newspaper she'd bought. She couldn't remember the last time she'd actually bought a recent paper. She smiled at the thought of how she used to read some of those old newspapers she'd kept at home, from time to time, just to remind her of the good old days. But they'd all gone along with everything else, to the dump now, she realised ruefully.

She'd also taken some money out of the hole-in-the-wall, just in case Clegg decided to put a stop on her access to funds. Although, until he got the bill from the credit card company, he wouldn't know how much she was spending. At least she'd been of sound enough mind to buy a return ticket so she could get home again, whatever else she chose to do next.

She thought about her friend, Mabel, who'd been in her and Jocelyn's clique at school but whom she hadn't seen in over thirty-five years, despite cards and photos they usually exchanged each Christmas.

Gloria could hardly believe it had been that long since Gerard, Mabel's husband, had moved them and their three children to Lincolnshire when he'd lost his job, in manufacturing. Luckily a cousin who lived there had got him a job where Gerard helped manage a vegetable and cereal farm of some seven hundred acres, outside Skegness, complete with a small cottage; although, of course, he must've retired long ago by now.

Initially, Mabel had worked as a seamstress but her arthritis eventually put paid to that, and she'd stayed home with the children and kept house. It didn't seem she'd had much of a life but then Gloria realised her *own* life hadn't been much of anything until this recent escapade.

So Gloria was nervously excited at the prospect of seeing her only other friend, after such a long time. And what an adventure, going there by herself! She hadn't been on a train since the Nineties with Arthur. Yet another thing, Gloria thought sadly, that she hadn't done for years.

The letter she'd written before leaving and given to Jocelyn, to stick through Clegg's letterbox, had been devised by the three of them. It was amazing how much time it had taken to write that one short letter. But she'd wanted the wording to create just the right impression. It was time she put her foot down on her son's hurtful antics.

My dear Clegg and Val,

I can't stand all the arguing that's been going on for years. And why? What did I ever do to make you treat me the way you have?

Anyway I'm going away for a while to think about things. Do not come after me and do not hound my dearest friends Jocelyn and Tilsbury. I will come back when I'm ready and not at your insistence.

And, Clegg, DO NOT EVEN THINK ABOUT SELLING
MY HOUSE UNTIL I GET BACK!!!
It is NOT yours to sell.

Your loving mother, Gloria xxx

Gloria giggled when she imagined their incensed indignation as they read those cutting words . . .

Chapter 16

Clouds, threatening rain, were lying low and a nippy wind was blowing when Gloria stepped from the train onto the platform at Skegness railway station, later that day. She felt dog-tired but it was that time of day when day-trippers were leaving so it was extremely busy and chaotic with children running around, people shouting and car horns blaring.

She ambled out of the station to look for a taxi. There was a rank right outside but lots of people queuing. The last thing Gloria felt like doing was to queue for hours on end when all she wanted to do was either sit down or go to bed. Plus she couldn't stand on her feet for too long these days. Old age, she thought, wearily. But she was hungry too.

So Gloria decided to take a stroll across the road, to look for somewhere to get a bite to eat first. Then she'd go back and see if the taxi queue had diminished.

She walked under the curly 'Welcome to Skegness' sign, past a statue of a sort of cartoon character called the Jolly Fisherman, dragging a suitcase not unlike hers! She found a little café, halfway up Skegness High Street and went in and ordered scrambled eggs and cheese on toast and a cup of tea.

Ordinary, plain food was such a joy after years of semi-warm potato soup.

She'd never been to Skeggy before and asked someone where the sea was.

'Right at the top of this road, love. Not far,' answered the young woman.

Well, she thought she might just go look at the sea because she was only going to be here for one night before going to find Mabel. The friendly staff at the hotel in Sheringham had also helped her book a one-night stay in a Skegness hotel, too.

The two post-Victoriana towns she'd visited in the last two days had a slightly tired feel about them. Just like me, she thought, at this moment in time. But, nevertheless, they clearly appealed to large numbers of people, judging by the masses of holidaymakers in both.

She passed cheap gift shops, an outdoor market and rock shops with rock shaped liked pebbles or, worse, dog poo! She chuckled, supposing that kids might like all that. And she recognised the proud clock tower from postcards Mabel had sent her, as well as the new-looking aquarium. Gloria took her time, looking around as she walked. Her new shoes didn't chafe, thankfully. She noted that what that young lady classed as 'not far' was actually a good walk away. But Gloria was determined to see the sea.

When she got there, panting a little, she could see that the beach went on for miles but the North Sea, here, looked a grim grey-brown colour in comparison to the sea around Sheringham. Or was that because the sun wasn't shining on it today?

Gloria sat on a bench and took a scarf out of her small case. It was chillier than she'd expected, despite feeling hot and bothered from her walk to the sea.

She tied the scarf neatly around her neck and sucked in three deep breaths of fresh air. Mabel was right. It was certainly brisk and bracing here.

A man was throwing a stick for his dog on the beach. It kept running back to him and dropping the stick at his feet, staring eagerly up at his master, panting, hoping – each time – for more, more, more. She'd got a little rescue dog when Clegg was small. A brown mongrel. They'd called it Rusty. He'd had tons of energy. Much like this one. Gloria smiled at his frolics and gazed in awe at the big white wind turbines, of the wind farms, out on the sea's horizon.

'Adult windmills.' She grinned.

It was a shame it wasn't sunny. Gloria looked at her watch and saw it was getting a little late to be wandering around a new town by herself. Grudgingly, she got to her feet, stopping to stretch as she felt a creak in her left hip. She rubbed it. She'd been far too active, of late, for an old woman of seventy-nine. Or was this was just her body adjusting to all the shenanigans she was getting up to?

Taking her time to meander back down the street, stopping periodically to look in shop windows, she made her way slowly back to the taxi rank. She was pleased she'd decided to have a cursory look round before getting straight into a taxi.

'Yeah but I'm knackered now,' she said out loud to herself.

Aha! No queue! Just as she'd hoped. The taxi rank was now empty, apart from a youngster with a backpack, staring at his phone.

The taxi dropped her off at the small hotel she'd booked, which was just perfect for her. No rowdy tourists. Just a couple of old dears in the bar, so Gloria said hello to them as she passed but went straight upstairs for an early night. She fell asleep as soon as her head touched the pillow.

The next morning, Gloria asked the taxi driver, from the night before, to drop her at her friend's house and wait outside for her, in case Mabel wasn't in. She'd memorised her address from the years and years of letters that had sped across the countryside to each other's doors.

It was a twenty-five-minute journey through a flat, bland landscape of huge fields surrounded by dykes that stretched for miles and miles in every direction. Ah but it was so lovely to see so much uncluttered space! When they arrived at the farm, the taxi drove slowly around the back, while Gloria looked for Mabel's home. They stopped outside a small white-washed stone cottage. Gloria eased herself out of the taxi and knocked on the door.

Nothing.

She began to wonder if this was the wrong place, although

the name of Mabel's house was on a post by the drive outside the main farmhouse. And there didn't seem to be any other buildings behind the farmhouse. She knocked louder, and heard a rustling movement when she put her ear to the door. Someone was in there.

What a relief!

Gloria stood there grinning, excitedly. She couldn't wait to see her old best friend from school days. A few minutes later a very surprised yet dishevelled Mabel answered the door. Gloria waved to the taxi driver.

'Gloria Frensham? It can't be! But oh my goodness, it is! It really is! I think we last exchanged photos in the Naughties, didn't we? Oh, I can't believe it! Well, what a marvellous surprise! Come in. Come in. You're staying I take it? Well, you wouldn't want to be coming all the way from Norfolk without staying, would you, my love?'

Gloria hugged her for a long time.

'Indeed I wouldn't, my dear, dear friend. And – oh – you virtually look the same, you do! Just a few flecks of grey in your hair . . .'

'More than a few, I'd say, Gloria. And, well, I must say you pretty much look the same but just a few inches around your midriff . . .'

They both burst out laughing.

'Ha, ha. Well the years haven't been too bad, I suppose. Now let me put the pan on for tea and you can tell me all your news!'

Mabel freed herself from Gloria's hug with a wheeze. She leaned on a stick, Gloria noted, and walked with a limp. Gloria had also noticed how skinny and frail Mabel was, when she'd hugged her, and how her dress hung loosely off her bony shoulders.

But the biggest shock was when Gloria looked beyond Mabel, into the space she, undoubtedly, called home.

Chapter 17

Seeing inside Mabel's little cottage for the first time was like déjà vu, for Gloria. It was exactly like her own house had been: stuff *everywhere*! Mainly newspapers and magazines. But in a much smaller, more claustrophobic and foul-smelling fusty, dirty environment. *Is this what people saw, then, when they first entered my house?* It must have been! The shock sent a little shiver down Gloria's spine.

She tried not to gag.

There was hardly any space to walk between the door and the one two-seater settee, opposite a blackened fireplace in the front room. Gloria couldn't see a TV, although a jingle came from a radio somewhere. Mabel's 'thing', Gloria could see, was newspapers and not just in piled-up heaps that were easy to get around either. It looked as though someone had been in and pulled the individual faded sheets out, one at a time, then bunched them up or torn them and strewn them all over the room. It was chaotic and baffling. And Mabel smelt as damp as the room itself.

Mabel noted the look of consternation on Gloria's face.

'My daughter made this mess of my newspapers yesterday.

She doesn't come to see me often,' she said quietly, with tears in her eyes. 'Said I should be ashamed of myself living like this.'

Gloria's mouth popped open in shock. 'Oh my God, Mabel. How awful for you!'

Mabel shook her head and moved painfully to the settee, plopping down with another wheeze. Gloria could see she would not be able to get up again easily. What a dreadful situation for her friend to have to tolerate. It filled Gloria with despair. Thank God she'd got out of her own house before desperation set in. And thank God for the good people at Green's Nursing Home, who'd helped her see that she could not go on living like that.

Seeing Mabel's house made Gloria determined never to go back to how she'd been living. And she knew she had to try and help Mabel, somehow.

'Right!' said Gloria, putting her suitcase down by the door and removing her jacket.

'Tell me where the kitchen is and I'll put the tea on. No, don't move. Just stay where you are, Mabel. I've got this.'

'Kitchen's next door. Um, bit of a mess in there, too, I'm afraid, and you might not find much. I, er, I haven't been eating lately you see. Don't need to eat so much now I'm at home all day.'

That last sentence piqued Gloria. She'd heard this excuse before. She'd used it herself with Clegg, on one of his visits, when she'd been feeling particularly sorry for herself, before

Tilsbury moved in to help her out more. Life had been getting harder and harder and yet Clegg had never even thought to ask how she was coping when it was patently clear, *without hindsight*, according to Green's Nursing Home, that her hoarding had 'consumed her' and 'very nearly killed her' as well.

Anyway, Mabel's kitchen seemed to be behind the fireplace. There were no doors. The sink was full of old chipped cups and dirty plates and dishes that looked as though they'd been there a very long time. There was no dishcloth, no tea towel, no bin. A pile of dirty clothes sat in an unruly heap, next to the only kitchen unit that housed the sink. There was an old gas stove that also looked as though it hadn't been used in decades. But no fridge.

However, when Gloria turned the tap, she was delighted to see that clean cold water actually came out of it.

'Mabel, how do you heat the water?'

'In a pan. There's an electric two-ring portable hob on one of the shelves. My Roy bought me that after Gerard died.'

Gloria had another déjà vu moment about heating water in a saucepan. I'm not the only one, she thought wryly. But she intended to be very careful this time.

'Gerard died? I didn't know that, Mabel.'

'He died this March. Freak farming incident with a tractor. He was showing a young chap the ropes. He wanted to retire you see. Well, he was seventy-eight. I'd wanted him to give it up years ago, as he should have done. But he loved it, you see, so he kept going. Anyway, the bloke reversed the tractor into him. Said he didn't see him.'

'Good Lord, Mabel!'

'Aye. It was terrible at the time. Luckily my Roy was around then and he sorted the funeral out and got me a few bits. You see, I've, er, been laid up quite a while now. Gerard was looking after me. Sandie was better to me back then. She doesn't understand me now. I'm okay apart from my aches and pains. Got a bit of tummy trouble, now. But I'm okay. Don't see my David much, but he gets me a few bits and pieces from time to time when I ask him to. He's got a guesthouse in Skeggy, you know.'

'Yes, you said in one of your letters. Doin' well by the sounds of it. Mabel, is the electric safe?'

'I think so. Made tea yesterday anyways.'

Gloria tentatively flicked the switch, expecting a loud bang! But, luckily, nothing happened. Moving things around on the shelves, stacked with old cereal boxes and other packaging from foodstuffs and the like, Gloria finally found some teabags but there was no milk. She washed two of the better-looking cups under the cold water tap.

Gloria had never tried tea without milk but she was determined to put on a poker face for her friend who, it was clear, was in *dire* need of some kind of support. She couldn't believe Mabel's three children had left her to live like this. At least, between them, Clegg and Tilsbury had made sure she had the basics.

Gloria was also shocked to note that there was no other food, whatsoever, in this very dilapidated tiny cottage, apart from half a bag of mouldy bread. And it looked as though Mabel had been picking off the mould and eating what was left, judging by the leftovers she'd found on one of the shelves.

Beyond the kitchen, Gloria spotted the small shower room and toilet. But it was filthy and there was a hole in one corner, straight through to the outside. Weeds had found their way in and insects were crawling around. The toilet pan itself was blackened with a dark green slime. She had no idea if any of it worked and felt saddened by Mabel's absolutely appalling predicament.

'Mustn't cry! Mustn't get upset. For Mabel's sake!' she told herself.

She tottered back into the lounge area with their hot drinks.

'So how've you been coping since Gerard's death, Mabel? I can see things have lapsed and, I hope you don't mind me sayin', but we do need to do a bit of sortin' out round here. You can't live like this, ducks,' she said, sitting down on the worn, uncomfortable settee next to her friend.

She sipped the weak brown liquid and was surprised it was not as bitter as she'd anticipated.

'Yes well it ain't been easy, my love. Gerard's death was a huge blow, of course. But the farm said I could live out my days here, rent-free. And I, um, know it ain't much to look at, Gloria, but it's home, at least.'

'Uh-huh. What've you got upstairs? Couple of bedrooms?'

'Yes just the two. Me and Gerard squashed into the little one and we let the kids share the larger one.'

'So how's life been since you left Norfolk?' Gloria asked, as she glanced around and processed Mabel's dreadful situation.

'Well, like I said in my postcards, David, Roy and Sandie all left home the minute they turned eighteen. Not surprising really. Not so much room here but this place and the job came at a time when we lost everything in Norfolk, as you know. It saved us in a way. I rarely hear from our Roy and see him even less. He's always been a bit of a hippy. Likes travelling around but never settled down. Lost his long-term girlfriend to cancer and it shook him up, it did. Never been the same since. Hadn't seen or heard from him in eight years. But then he popped back a few days before Gerard died, fortunately, and helped me out a bit and then shot off again after the funeral. Never rings.

'And, well, Sandie got married and lived near our David in Skeggy for a while. But she split up with her husband and moved back to Norwich. Didn't have any kids with him. But she married one of her old boyfriends and they've got a daughter, Chloe. In fact, Sandie's a grandmother now. Chloe got pregnant at fifteen and the boyfriend didn't want to know; all of which I think was a shame. But she lives at home with our Sandie. At least that's the reason my daughter gives for not being able to come up and see me much.'

'Hmm. Right. So you have a phone? Can you ring her if you need to?'

Mabel nodded. 'It's one of the few things that works in this house, my love. Ha, ha! Phone's by the door on the window ledge. Small pad there with Sandie and David's numbers. David pays for it.'

'Well that's a blessing then,' Gloria said cheerily and eased herself, with difficulty, out of the old settee.

'Right well I want you to sit there and relax, Mabel, and I'm going to do some sorting out around here. No, I don't want you to worry about things. I'm doing this, and I need to know how to get hold of the farmer – and also when's bin day?'

Chapter 18

Gloria couldn't remember the last time she'd done a full day's housework. Or perhaps it had been when Arthur was alive and there'd been space around the telly and getting up to the bathroom had been a whole lot easier. But as her hoarding had gradually crept over all the available floor space and risen up the walls, eventually blocking the hoover, cleaning products and her clothes in cupboards and wardrobes, all thoughts of trying to clean the place or live a so-called normal life evaporated.

Yet, despite her own hoarding tendencies, Gloria could clearly see that Mabel's cottage was a disgrace and completely unfit for anyone to live in, whereas at least Gloria's own home had been mould-free and watertight. But her immediate worry was that the state of this place was taking its toll on Mabel. She'd tried to ring the farmer but was informed he was at a country fayre for a few days. Pah! And if the farmer thought he was getting off lightly by not helping with Mabel's predicament he was soon going to learn the error of his ways!

Gloria successfully boiled that pan a lot over the next few hours – so no more burns to her hands!

She started on the bathroom and then moved into the kitchen. She found an old scrubbing brush at the back of the only cupboard. There were no other cloths, so the brush would have to do. And looking in the many discarded bottles of empty cleaning fluids she managed to accumulate just enough of the remains, although some of it was too hard. She mixed it with water to form a liquidy cleaning paste of sorts and set to, cleaning the downstairs areas as best she could. At least she thought it would make everything smell a whole lot nicer.

From time to time Mabel would call out from the lounge. 'Here, Gloria. What you doin' in the kitchen?'

Or: 'Do you need some help?'

'Never you mind what I'm doin', ducks. Now just rest and put yer feet up. I'm just doin' a bit of clearing up to make yer life a wee bit easier. And no arguments. Read one of your newspapers or summat!'

That made Mabel smile.

Broken or unusable crockery she put into boxes and she'd put all the other rubbish into old plastic carrier bags. She'd found those when rooting about, amongst all Mabel's stuff. The exertion was knackering and her back and hip were playing up but she was determined to finish the tasks she'd set herself, in order to help her friend.

She paused at one point to wonder what would have happened to her, at the end of the day, if that electrical fault hadn't occurred? Would anyone have tried to rescue her, like she was attempting to rescue Mabel from her dreadful fate?

She remembered Val trying to do that once but Gloria had been outraged, back then. Regretfully, she realised now, she perhaps should have been thankful.

Gloria returned to the slow and sometimes painful process, especially when she bent down to remove a dead mouse and then nearly couldn't pull herself back up. She'd had to sit on the filthy tiled floor and get her breath back and then pull herself up, gradually, on the edge of the sink unit.

'C'mon, old girl!' she encouraged herself.

She was tired and hungry yet there was nothing in the place to eat; nothing at all. But she wanted to keep going because she knew once she stopped for the day she might never get started again. At least she'd had a good fry-up at the guesthouse before she left to come and find Mabel, which was clearly more than Mabel had eaten in quite a while.

After she'd sorted the kitchen and bathroom out as best she could, she opened the kitchen window because it was the only one that would open. A light breeze came skipping in and began dispelling some of the damp and foul odours that had clearly accumulated and hung in the air like rancid drains, over the years.

At the end of that first day, Gloria had cleaned and scrubbed and cleared all the rubbish out of the kitchen and cleaned and removed the weeds and insects from the bathroom. Oh, no doubt they'd return at some point. But this was just a quick clear-up to get Mabel sorted out.

After helping Mabel up from the sofa and assisting her to

remove her clothing, Gloria encouraged her friend to have a wash-down. Unfortunately, only cold water trickled out of the shower. Gloria handed over tiny pieces of soap she'd found on the small window ledge, near the hole in the bathroom.

'I'm sorry it's only cold water, Mabel. But I've put warm water in the sink for you to use too. So try and make do with that as best you can, love. You deserve to have a proper shower and I'm going to make sure you get one very soon. But for now will you be okay with this? We need to keep clean at our age. I remember the first time I had a bath, recently, after many years of just using a bathroom sink. And it was marvellous, I can tell you.'

It pained Gloria that Mabel only nodded in a sad response.

'I'll go find you a towel.'

The only towel Gloria could find was stained and damp but that couldn't be helped. Under the circumstances, it would have to do. Mabel looked very frail standing there waiting for the towel. Gloria tried not to stare at her bony ribs and loose skin and attempted to hide tears that sprang to her eyes. She found Mabel's nightie upstairs in her tiny, fusty, damp bedroom and brought it down for her friend. Then she helped her friend up the narrow stairs to bed and returned downstairs to boil the pan once again to make her friend more tea. Then she tiredly climbed the rickety stairs for the third time that day, clinging on to the dodgy handrail, tea sloshing over the sides of the chipped cup she was carrying.

'You've done me proud, Gloria. But I . . . I didn't want you to see me like this. And you shouldn't be working at your time of life.'

Gloria was completely shattered, perspiring and out of breath. The dress she was wearing was smeared with grime. But she'd kept her face plastered with encouraging smiles, throughout the day, for Mabel's benefit. What a horrible way for her poor friend to live, she thought, sadly. But she wasn't going to say that to Mabel. So Gloria shook her head.

'I'm not working, Mabel. I'm helping out my dear friend. You might be surprised to learn that I've had the very same troubles myself recently. And I've finally had some help gettin' through it. So I'm just helping you out, too. We do what we can, Mabel, when someone's in need. Age has got nowt to do with it. So don't go worryin' yourself about that, ducks.'

Mabel fell asleep as soon as her head touched the pillow. Soft snoring could be heard as Gloria closed her friend's door and removed her teacup.

After she'd put Mabel to bed Gloria had poked her head into the kids' bedroom.

'Bloody hell, Mabel!' She grimaced, her eyes widening.

The ceiling was in a state of collapse along the top of one wall. You could see the pale summer sky beyond, just like in the bathroom. A steady drip, drip of accumulated rainwater could be seen in one corner that had drenched the children's beds and soaked the rotting carpet. There was a blackish slimy mould down the walls and all over the bedcovers. It was also where the awful putrid decaying aroma was coming from, which permeated the whole house. Everything in that room would have to be removed and dumped. In fact, Gloria was horrified to realise that the whole house probably needed *demolishing*.

How could Mabel's children have left her to deteriorate in this awful environment? She felt furious with Mabel's son David, who was the one living closest to her and yet had done nothing to help. But the others hadn't bothered to help either. Pah! There was *no* excuse for how they'd treated her.

Gloria made her way back down the rickety stairs and stepped outside to gulp the fresh country air into her lungs. She sat on a milk churn by the front door and savoured the peace and quiet for a moment, feeling greedy for the fresh, clean air. She couldn't *believe* Mabel's predicament could be this bad. *Oh, the joys of getting old and not being able to do things for yourself!*

It was still light and a misty sun hung low in the sky, encouraging last-minute outings or adventures amongst the arcades and blinking lights of the Skegness waterfront should anyone wish to partake. Gloria was shattered after all her hard work and just wanted some shut-eye. Yet where would she sleep?

She wandered back into Mabel's stale, damp, oppressive little cottage and shut the door. She was still hot and clammy and badly needed a shower herself but she decided to go without. There was no way she would attempt to have one whilst she was here. Not having a bath or shower was what she'd been used to in her own house in Norwich, after all. So it wasn't really a big deal. However, now she'd experienced regular bathing she wanted to continue enjoying that privilege, wherever she ended up.

In the kitchen she simply washed her face with cold water then moved back into the front room and got down onto the hard floor with some difficulty. It took her a while to drag newspapers underneath her to fashion a bed and she pulled some loose sheets of it over her like Tilsbury had to do in her house. At least it was a warm night. *But what a way to live!*

She was also a little worried about what might be crawling around on the floor with her whilst she slept and that's even *if* she was able to sleep in these circumstances on such a hard scuffed dirty floor like this. But Gloria was so worn out that it didn't take her long to drift off and start snoring softly, herself.

Chapter 19

On the second day at poor Mabel's, Gloria got out the business card and rang her friendly taxi driver, Jim, and asked him to fetch eggs, butter, bread and a carton of long-life milk from the nearest shop. There was no way she could go another day without eating anything. And Mabel was wasting away, judging by her emaciated frame. She also asked Jim if he'd kindly remove and dump all the rubbish she'd managed to clear from the cottage.

She did chuckle to herself at that. 'Dump all the rubbish,' she'd said to Jim. A few days ago the very idea of dumping rubbish would've been preposterous to Gloria Frensham. But today, because of poor Mabel, she was thinking, *Thank God for bin days!*

'Of course, I'll pay you whatever the going rate is. But I'm helpin' my friend who's sick, you see. Her family have abandoned her and there's no one to help but me.'

Jim was far more accommodating than Gloria would have thought but then she'd already spent near on £44 with him already.

'Yeah, of course love. S'nice what you're doin'. D'you want

a hand with anything else while I'm here? Any liftin' or getting summat down from somewhere?'

'No, ducks. It's all done now. Thanks!'

There was no way Gloria could sort out all the stacked newspapers but the stuff Sandie had thrown around in dismay had now gone and so had a lot of other crap from around Mabel's home. At least the kitchen was cleaner now, the shelves emptied of rubbish, the loo pan was whitish again and the shower room could be used, once you got used to the cold water. A bit of elbow grease had done wonders. Plus there was a bit more space around the lounge and she'd even found the radio.

Gloria got Mabel downstairs to use the loo and then discovered there was no more toilet paper. Luckily she had tissues in her tiny suitcase, which then found a new home. Afterwards Gloria encouraged Mabel to eat scrambled eggs, a piece of buttered bread and a cup of tea *with milk*. It all tasted grand and even Mabel nodded a grateful thank you to Gloria, her mouth full of eggs. The food would last a couple of days at least. Gloria just wanted to get Mabel's resolve and strength back before she sorted anything else out. She could see Mabel was fading now Gerard had gone and now that Sandie was behaving like a spoilt brat, even though the woman was in her late forties.

After their meal, Gloria helped Mabel get dressed and persuaded her to come outside for a little walk seeing as it was such a nice sunny day. She wanted to get Mabel's limbs moving because Gloria could see that walking wasn't a pastime Mabel was too familiar with these days. A light wind breezed in through the open window.

'We'll take it slow, ducks. Here's your stick. But show me around the place, Mabel. I've never been on a farm before.'

Gloria could see that Mabel was brighter than yesterday and she even had a cheery smile pasted on her lips today, although it took them a while to get going. The barn behind Mabel's cottage that stored the cereals was vast. The flat Lincolnshire countryside around here was bare and stark, perfect for growing crops but devoid of any character. There were few trees apart from those framing the main farmhouse.

But Gloria was stiff from her walk to the Skegness seafront and all her hard work yesterday at Mabel's. And Mabel's pained gait slowed them down even further. They probably only went some twenty yards before Mabel said she wanted to go back. She sat down on the milk churn to get her breath back.

'Gerard used to sit on this to take his boots off,' she murmured. 'But, you know, I never walk anywhere or do anything really.'

'Yes I can see that, Mabel. But doesn't David ever come and take you out? And is Sandie always so darned trouble-some?'

'They don't bother with me, now. David can't really get away in the summer because it's peak season in Skeggy. His wife, Fi, does most of it. Their Rebecca left home and went to

London as a dancer. Been dancin' all her life. Started at the Embassy on the front – I might have told you. Doesn't come home much. You see, they're all so busy now. So I . . . I don't like to bother them, Gloria.'

Gloria's growing annoyance because of the situation had been kept in check whilst she'd been Mabel's guest. Yet she wasn't usually one to hold her feelings back, especially anguish. She felt it bubbling to the surface, now.

'Well I'm sorry, Mabel, but from what you've told me, I can't accept all this tiptoeing around. I've had the same sort of problems myself, with me own family, and it's not a good situation to be in. Plus you can't survive on your own out here with no help at all. Your lot have got to realise that.'

'But I told them I'm okay.'

'But you're not okay, Mabel. When was the last time you ate summat proper?'

Mabel looked sad. 'Um, well –'

Gloria softened. She saw herself in Mabel. She, too, had pooh-poohed all offers of help in the past and it hadn't done her any good. It had even given Clegg some leverage when he came to move her out of her own house that day. No wonder he thought the only solution was to put her in an old people's home. She could suddenly see how he'd reached that decision.

Gloria helped Mabel back indoors and onto the settee. She proceeded to make them a cup of tea, while deep in thought.

'I'd like to help you, Mabel, if you'll let me. You can't carry on living here like this and Sandie and David need to be told. The farmer probably also has a responsibility to you as well. A run-down cottage ain't compensation for nothing. So will you let me help you?'

'But *how* can you help me?'

Gloria could see Mabel was a proud woman but it hadn't worked in her favour. Her ruddy kids had clearly turned a blind eye to her situation. But perhaps they'd turned a blind eye because they weren't sure what to do about it? Green's Nursing Home had opened Gloria's eyes by telling her how families often worried about how to look after their aged parents at the end of their lives.

Possibly Mabel's family didn't have the *time* to do anything about it? Or probably they were worried about who Mabel would live with? Or, if they decided to put her into a home, who would take on the responsibility for that decision? There were a lot of considerations with issues like this, Gloria suddenly realised.

'Okay. Well, what I'd like to do, if you're okay with this, is ring both David and Sandie, tonight, and tell them what's been going on. I'll tell them I think you probably need to have a check-up with your doctor and social services will need to see how you've been living. You're not able to get around very well any more, so you might have to consider going to live with one of your kids or moving into a home where you can get proper support.

'I went into a nursin' home for a while and the lovely people there helped me no end. David and Sandie can help you do that and maybe the farmer owes you some compensation too. However, that's for David and Sandie to sort out. But I'm sure you'll agree that something needs to be done. You cannot carry on living like this, Mabel. This house isn't fit for human habitation and it's making you ill. Would you be happy for me to do that?'

Mabel hung her head low. She sniffed and Gloria realised she was quietly crying.

'I d-didn't want it to come to this, Gloria. I thought I could cope. But things've been getting steadily w-worse day by day.'

Gloria put her arms around her friend.

'There, there. I know, love. But you've got to look after yourself and if *you* can't, then you've got to let other people do that for you. That's how it is when we get older, as I'm finding out myself. Besides it can't be much fun living here by yourself without Gerard. Remember how he wanted the best for you all? He worked hard for that, didn't he? He'd be upset to see you like this, now, wouldn't he, love? And he'd *still* want the best for you before you join him in the never-never. I've got the same decisions to make myself, when I goes back, too, Mabel. Happens to us all in the end, ducks. S'never plain sailing, life, is it?'

As she spoke those words to Mabel, the full truth of what she was saying hit home for Gloria as well. Yes, at some point in the not-too-distant future, she would have to go home and deal with all these unsavoury aspects of her own life, too. It was totally depressing. But she wasn't going to tell Mabel that.

'Tell you what, Mabel, let's have a nice little cup of tea, and a chat about old times now, shall we?'

Chapter 20

Gloria guessed her phone calls would be met with objections, when she spoke to David and Sandie, later that day. Indeed, at first they both yelled at her, which was unnerving and the word 'busybody' was even mentioned! But she held her ground and put her point across, calmly. She said she'd stay with Mabel until they both came to see exactly how she'd been living but that she wouldn't be able to stay any longer than a couple of days when she had to get back to her own family.

Sandie flatly said she wouldn't be able to come up again until the following week, due to work commitments but would come as soon as possible after that. She said David would have to sort things out by himself. David duly arrived early the next morning before Mabel was up. He informed Gloria that his wife was looking after the guesthouse, so he was able to be here. He'd calmed down by the time he set foot in the door but he could not look Gloria in the eye.

'She's your mam, David. Choose your poison, lad. She either comes to live with you or you have to find her a good home. It's what your dad would expect of ya, son.'

She could see David was embarrassed by the whole situation. Understandably.

'I know. I know. Er, I'm sorry I shouted at you, Mrs Frensham. Bit shocked about all this, that's all. Sis can't get her head around it either. And I don't think she wants to deal with it. So I'll have to. And I don't mean that in a bad way. Um I guess I knew that one day things would come to a head. But we've all been so busy. Never realised just how bad things were here, I guess. Or maybe we didn't *want* to see how things've been with Mum. So thanks for being here, Gloria. Don't like to think what could've happened to her without your being here. So, um, can I give you a lift somewhere?'

'Well, lad, I hadn't thought about leavin' so soon. Really wanted to stay until I knew someone was steppin' up. But I guess that's what you're doin', now, lad. Did you speak to social services?'

Mabel's apologetic son shook his head.

'No, sorry, I haven't. I wanted to swing by and see what's been happening here first. And it's crap, I can see that, now. I would've come sooner but the guesthouse is always full in the summer. And, sure, I can see you think we've all neglected her. And you're right; we have. But look. What I'm thinking is this: I'd like to take her back to the guesthouse tomorrow but I can't do that today. We've no spare rooms. But I've got a cancellation tomorrow for two weeks, so Mum could have that room, as an interim arrangement. It's a lovely room with a sea view so that'll be nice for her. But – er – I don't really like to ask, but with you being her friend and all, I'm just wondering if you could possibly stay with her again tonight. Could you do that?'

Gloria nodded. 'Yep I'd prefer that. It'll give her time to say goodbye to the place. All her memories are here, too. But can you get her a doctor's appointment as soon as? Just to get her checked out. She might have problems with her stomach, she told me.'

David agreed that he would take responsibility for his mother's welfare from now on, including having a word with the farmer.

So Gloria spent her last evening with Mabel, chatting about their lives and actually having a laugh, despite the dire situation. She was relieved everything would be all right for her dear old friend now. Well, she sincerely hoped it would be. She told Mabel she'd give her a ring in a few days' time, once she was established at David's, and also wrote down her son's phone number for Mabel, in case she wanted to call any time.

When David came to collect them after breakfast, the following morning, Mabel had chosen only to bring an old photo album with her and Gerard's fishing rod, which she gave to David. Everything else she could've taken with her was mouldy or broken or under piles of magazines. She left all her damp clothes in the wardrobe. The crockery and cutlery belonged to the cottage as did all the furnishings so there was really little else to take.

'It's going to be a new start for me, from now on, thanks

to you, Gloria. And I do thank you with all my heart,' Mabel said, a happy smile gracing her tired face, as she hugged her best friend.

Gloria then picked up her tiny suitcase and breathed a sigh of relief. She was glad to be leaving that dire, oppressive little cottage of Mabel's.

Everybody then got into David's BMW and they all left together for Skegness station, without looking back.

Once she'd settled down on the train, thankful to be leaving Skegness for her journey back to Norfolk that day, Gloria again thought about the parallels between Mabel's story and her own predicament. She wiped away a tear as the conductor asked to see her ticket. It was so difficult for everyone concerned, she thought, when an elderly relative needed caring for.

But now she'd seen and fully understood, first-hand, how impactful and disruptive these decisions were on everyone's lives. And she could see how depression could easily sweep through a person's life and stop them caring about looking after themselves and their home properly.

Gloria reinforced her vow to Green's Nursing Home, there and then, that she would NEVER start hoarding things ever again. Plus, from seeing the sad, emaciated physical state of Mabel, she knew she must look after herself, physically and mentally, in order to remain healthy.

She'd also need to be more accepting of Clegg and Val's concerns about her welfare from now on. And even though she fought against it, she knew the day would come when she'd have to be accepting of their decision to put her in an old people's home. She now realised it was nothing to do with them not loving her. It was to do with the logistics of it all.

Christ! It was so distressing being old and infirm.

The duh-duh-duh-duh of the train lulled her into a relaxed state. She gazed out the window at the scenery speeding by, thinking she might just have a nap.

But by the time Gloria's train had reached Grantham she'd had another impetuous thought and decided to get off there and board another train. This time for London.

'Well, I don't think I'm ready for an old people's home just yet and I've never been to London!' she declared to a pigeon that was obliviously pecking at crumbs along the grey platform.

Chapter 21

Oh, Tilsbury!

She wished he was here with her. She'd only been gone a few days but it felt like a lifetime ago when they'd bathed together in the sea, somewhere down the coast from Sheringham. It had been such fun and such a contrast to her time spent with Mabel, which had been upsetting and bleak. She desperately hoped David would look after his mother now. He'd promised he would. He'd also *promised* that she would have the room with a sea view for two weeks until they could sort out the best arrangement for her.

How lovely for Mabel to see the sea every day! What a treat.

But – oh – London!

The bustle; the colour; the crazy, exhilarating ambience. Black taxis. Red buses. Silver buses – were those *silver* buses? Buses with all manner of flashing advertisements daubed over them. Flags. Tall, imposing buildings and massive shops with glitz and glamour. People from all walks of life, scurrying along as though they had somewhere important to go. Vehicles crowding the roads; pedestrians crowding the pavements. A large plane soaring overhead. The underground with its confusing warren of tunnels. And a helpful little man who told her what an Oyster card was and showed her where to get one.

It was like being given total freedom to explore the city . . .

She didn't ring Clegg about her London trip and as far as she knew he hadn't the foggiest about the Skegness trip either. Last time she looked, this was *her* adventure!

When she came out of King's Cross station and before she went anywhere else she made her way into a brightly coloured café. She was hungry and didn't want to be walking far, not knowing where the heck she was, with hunger pangs stabbing at her belly.

'Here, ducks. I'll have one of them sandwiches, there. What you got?'

'Well they're not really sandwiches, ma'am. They're chicken burgers.'

'Ooo. I've heard of them. All the kiddies eat 'em now don't they?'

'Do you want to eat in, lady, or take out?'

'Well I'd like to sit a while before I go off sightseeing. Is that okay?'

The youngster nodded with a smile. 'Order and pay here and then go take a seat anywhere. This your first time to London?'

'Oh yes and it will be my last, if you know what I mean! Ha, ha. But don't worry, I'm having fun!' Gloria said with a twinkle in her eye.

She thought the food was tasty if a little salty and she drank tea from a paper cup; afterwards, just sitting, watching the world go by in a colourful, noisy blur; feeling excited about her latest adventure.

Then clutching her small trusty suitcase, Gloria made her way back into the station, amongst the jostling throngs of tourists, to where people were feeding their tickets into the gate slots, which then opened to let them through for the underground. She did the same and then asked to be shown which tube to get on to take her to Big Ben. It was such an iconic landmark and of all the places she could visit in the capital, Big Ben and the Houses of Parliament was where she most wanted to go.

She finally came out of Westminster tube station, having asked lots of people where to go and getting lots of help – and there was the sight she'd been dying to see: Big Ben. She cricked her neck looking up at it. At the intricately patterned tower with gold decorations. Was it real gold? There were narrow windows beneath the clock face, too. She'd never noticed those before on the telly. And somewhere inside the Houses of Parliament, she knew, MPs were plotting and planning and revising the laws of the land.

Oh, but London was magnificent! It was so thrilling just being there; being part of the throng and buzz of everyday life in that huge city. Of course, it was tiring too, yes, but oh so exciting.

'My dear Tilsbury. It's a shame you and Jocelyn can't be

here, ducks. It's just magical. This is just one of the best things I've ever done in me life. Well, apart from our trip to the seaside, of course!' she said to the sky; to the other tourists around her; to the light breeze, whipping deftly through people's lives.

'They're places you see on the news all the time and, just think, *I've been there too now*!' she was going to tell them all when she got home.

But what could prove she'd actually been to London? What could she give everyone so they knew she'd truly been there, on her own, and had this amazing adventure? She'd never had a mobile phone like Clegg and his family, so she wasn't able to take photos or text or whatever people did. It had to be something more tangible.

Ah, yes! Easy-peasy! Ha, ha! She'd send them *postcards* from one of the souvenir vendors, like Mabel used to do! She'd have to choose specific postcards of Big Ben or with Big Ben somewhere in the photos, so everyone knew she'd *really* been to London.

Gloria found exactly what she was looking for in one of the souvenir shops back near King's Cross station, where she'd soon be ready to board her train for Grantham, in order to go back to Norwich.

'D'you sell stamps too? And I'll need to borrow a pen to write them. And is there a letterbox anywhere nearby?' she asked, holding four postcards in her hand.

Gloria was sending one to Clegg and Val, one to Jocelyn

and Marvin that she hoped Tilsbury would see, one to Green's Nursing Home and, of course, one to Mabel, care of her David, back in Skegness. And these postcards would serve two purposes:

'One, by saying, instead of a phone call, that I am alive and well and enjoying my solo adventures, all over the nation! And, two, to prove that I've ticked one of the must-see boxes off my new bucket list, which I've just invented. Top of the list – must see Big Ben! Done and dusted. Thank you very much!'

Chapter 22

Later that same evening, Gloria Frensham stared at her naked body in the full-length mirror in the hotel bedroom. She'd never ever looked at herself, properly, without any clothes on. She'd never had a full-length mirror to do that for one thing. Only the side light was on by the double-for-sole-occupancy bed. She couldn't bear to look at herself in full light. She felt rather risqué looking at herself like this, anyway!

It made her giggle to think of Tilsbury on the beach only a matter of days ago, running around in his birthday suit, without a care in the world! And why not? Their bodies weren't actually disgusting in any way. They just *hung* differently to when they were younger. There were a few creases and a bit of flab, too, of course. And they weren't so firm any more.

But as she looked more closely in the mirror, Gloria could see that it wasn't just the shape and look of her body nor even the scar from the caesarean she'd had bearing Clegg. It was the way she was holding herself that made her look despondent and sad.

Standing as she usually stood, she noted that her shoulders slouched. There was also resignation in her face. Too many knocks and not enough fun or parties, she realised. So it was her general *demeanour* that made her look old; made older people, she thought, *look* old.

'So *that's* it. That's why we're old!' she concluded. 'Youth and liveliness are down to always having something to look forward to. And unlimited energy. And never letting stuff get you down. Yep, I can see that now. Inner energy; an inner vibrancy!'

She realised she mainly felt so old because she didn't seem able to hold on to her own energy or joie de vivre for too long, now she was nearly eighty. Even all the positive, new things she was suddenly gleefully experiencing – since leaving her dull, empty life in her old house – seemed to slip away like the sand between her toes on the beach near Sheringham.

'So you always need something to look forward to,' she said slowly to her reflection in the mirror. 'You need a reason to get out of bed, old girl. And you need to keep making memories. Especially when you're an old fogey.'

Having booked into the Norwich city hotel for two nights was the best thing she could have done now, she realised. She wanted to have a long soak in a bath as well as a rest and wash her new but smelly clothing before going back to deal with Clegg and Val. She also wanted to have a jolly good think about things, after her madcap adventures in Sheringham with Tilsbury and the unsettling experience with Mabel, as well as careering round London's sights, all of which had been a marvellous, much-needed respite.

She knew she couldn't go on gallivanting about but she had no intention of going back to Clegg's until she was fully relaxed and completely ready to deal with her son. She wasn't quite ready to do that yet. He'd always been stubborn but he was also too strong for her to deal with at the moment.

She knew her resolve and energy had come and gone in waves over the last few days. One minute she'd felt ecstatic about what she'd been seeing or feeling and the next minute she'd plunged down to the depths, like when she saw how ill Mabel looked because of the way she was living. But at least she'd helped Mabel with her situation. She felt very proud of herself for that fact. Being out and about had – overall – been fantastic and liberating for Gloria but she was very tired now.

Well, maybe her tiredness was also partly because she knew she'd have to go back at some point. Back to Clegg and, ultimately, back to the realisation that sooner or later she'd have to go into an old people's home because she wouldn't always be able to manage her life by herself. It wasn't a thought she relished. But it was a truth she knew she'd have to acknowledge, just like Mabel would have to.

Maybe if Arthur had still been alive it wouldn't have seemed such a daunting process. She'd never envisioned Arthur dying in his fifties. She remembered back to when they'd just moved into the home she'd inherited and him saying, 'I'd love to grow old with you.'

Gloria chuckled at that thought. It was obviously said as a romantic gesture. They'd certainly never entertained thoughts of sitting together, staring out of the window, in an old people's home, when he made that statement.

Yet would any of her marvellous new experiences be a lasting, comforting memory – when she *was* wrapped up in the mundane ordinariness of the daily sitting around the edge of a soundless room with other tired old people, rarely visited by family – when that time came?

But it was pleasing that it got easier and easier to sleep when her head touched the pillow . . .

* * *

The next morning Gloria couldn't bring herself to get up or open the curtains or anything. She lay in bed, her eyes feeling heavy. She'd had a manic few days running around, when she never normally did anything of note. But – oh boy – did she still feel tired. She needed more sleep. And she would have a lie-in because she could. She drifted back to sleep.

It seemed, the next minute, someone was pounding on the door. She awoke, groggily. The chambermaid.

'Please! No! I'm here another night. You can do the room tomorrow. I, er, I'm not feeling well!' she said.

'Okay, ma'am.'

The chambermaid moved on to the next room, probably thinking she'd get to finish her shift early, for once.

Gloria snuggled back under the comfortable duvet and slept. Little did the chambermaid know that Gloria had turned over a new leaf. There'd practically be nothing for the chambermaid to do when she came back the next day because Gloria had tidied up after herself as she went along – all her clothes, now they'd dried, were folded neatly in her little suitcase and she'd even scrubbed the bath and basin clean, using one of the hotel flannels.

'Waahh!' Gloria yawned, as she awoke to the sun piercing through the tiny gap in the hotel curtains. The clock on the TV said 16:20. *Good Lord!*

'But I must've needed it, eh, room!'

She got up, opened the curtains, squinted as the afternoon sun bathed the room in a bright light, and ordered a sandwich from room service.

'Where to next, room?' she said, her mouth full of cheesy pickle and ham. Or should she while her remaining hours away watching hotel TV?

But perhaps it *was* time to go back now. There was nothing else she wanted to do right now; nothing specific; nothing else she wanted to see. Even her new bucket list sat empty in her heart. The London trip had been a whirlwind stunner and something she'd never envisaged she'd get to do. In fact, in these few short exhilarating, frenzied days she'd done everything her heart had desired. She was amazed she could have done all that without thinking about things in too much depth. She'd just needed to jump up and run off every which way. It had actually been that simple. Yet she was seventy-nine, for God's sake, soon to be eighty.

She'd never had a mid-life crisis before! *Or was it an end-of-life crisis?*

It had started with Tilsbury, taking her out for an innocent cream tea. But thank God he'd done that. It had saved her. It had also saved Mabel, she noted with pride. She hummed to herself, as she packed her remaining items.

But what the heck should she do next?

Chapter 23

'But it can't be, love. I only made one small call to my friend!'

The kindly receptionist did not pout or stamp her foot or stick her tongue out at the irate customer in front of her. She'd been trained not to. But Gloria was sure she would have *liked* to.

'I'm sorry, ma'am, but the hotel prices are listed in your room. And I know you say you only made a small call yesterday afternoon but it is always more expensive calling from hotel bedrooms.'

Gloria had only called to check that Mabel was settled with David or rather she'd called to *check up* on David's *promise* to make sure Mabel was settling in.

Mabel had been thrilled she'd called.

'Oh, yes, it's so lovely here, my love. I can see the sea and I've had a couple of champion meals down in the restaurant with all the other guests. It's been a real treat and just wonderful having so many other lovely people around me. Feel so much better already. And it feels like I'm on me holidays. I can't thank you enough for what you've done for me, Gloria!'

'Well, I just wanted to make sure you were all right, Mabel, you bein' my friend of so many years and all. Wanted to make sure your family did right by you, too. And have you spoken to Sandie yet or seen the doctor? Has David rung the farmer, d'you know?'

'Oh yes. I spoke to Sandie. She apologised, Gloria, and that's all I wanted really. She's coming up to see me and bringing Chloe and her kiddie at the weekend – only two days to go – so that'll be nice! And I've a doctor's appointment on the Monday. But I think David's been having problems with the farmer. Says he won't be threatened. But social services went down to the cottage and took photos of it. There'd been a leak in the kids' bedroom ceiling for ages and it caved in when social services went in there, poking around. So it looked even worse than when you were there.'

'Oh well that's good news. And it'll give social services some ammo to deal with the ruddy farmer as well then. What did David actually say to him?'

'Well he told him – dare I say it – that he was an arsehole and that a letter would be forthcoming from his solicitor, for treating me like that. Then he slammed the phone down. And my David's not usually one for outbursts of anger!'

'Oh well, I'm glad things are all sorted out for you now, ducks. You deserve some luck and good fortune now. Well, ducks, I hope you have a lovely time when your daughter's family finally arrive and I'll ring you again in a couple of weeks' time. Ta-ra, Mabel. Lots of love. Bye for now, ducks!'

'Thank you, Gloria. You take good care of yourself too. Bye now. Byeee.'

The hotel receptionist stated that Gloria's call had taken 7.48 minutes, which meant the bill was correct. The price of the phone call was £8.15 since calls were priced at £1.09 per minute.

'Cor blimey what a rip-off!'

Gloria reluctantly held out her credit card to pay for the sandwich and pricey phone call; £16.65 was debited, along with a further £118.00 for the room for two nights with breakfast. She was getting used to paying for everything by credit card, but she didn't dare to think how much she'd spent already.

Ah well, Clegg would soon start to put two and two together when he got his statement and her postcard arrived. Sheringham prices it wasn't.

Chapter 24

Gloria pressed her face up to the travel agency's window to get a better look at the holidays on offer. She was sheltering from the rain under their shop canopy, after leaving the Norwich hotel, unsure of where to go or what to do next.

She'd come out of the hotel, after paying her bill, and turned left and meandered down a couple of roads, until she'd come across this travel agency. Those idyllic photos of sun-drenched beaches with stone-skimmingly flat turquoise seas were *very* appealing and if she'd had the enthusiasm as well as the figure for a slinky bikini – and if she'd been in her forties again – she'd have jumped at the chance. But her skin had never liked intense heat. It made her all blotchy. And she'd never renewed her passport. So she wasn't going anywhere sultry, any time soon.

A light drizzle had started to fall but the shop's canopy was keeping her dry. Perhaps she should've thought to buy an umbrella in Sheringham, as well as her new clothes. Too late now. But she'd think about buying one today, if she could find somewhere that sold them.

The drizzle increased in intensity and so more people started to join her; also using this time to stare, longingly, into the travel agency's window. It was getting cramped under the canopy.

Perhaps that's why she suddenly found herself trying the door handle and walking through it before she realised what she was doing. She was the only person in there, apart from the clerks, busily typing at their desks.

'Not very nice out there now is it?' said one of the three smartly dressed young women, looking up.

Gloria shook her head. 'Yet we've had a lovely summer so far, don't ya think?' she replied.

She realised that now the young woman was in conversation with her, and the fact that she had actually stepped inside the shop, meant she was a potential customer.

'Why don't you take a seat and we can try and find somewhere nice for you to go?' The young woman smiled. There was a badge on her jacket that said 'Keri' on it.

Gloria did as she was told and plopped herself onto the nicely padded blue seat.

'Would you like a cup of tea or coffee or a glass of water?' Keri asked.

'Why yes, ducks. That would be nice. Tea, milk no sugar thanks.'

Gloria was also vaguely aware that by accepting a drink she was, probably, being ensnared by the travel agency employee. She noticed a sign nearby that said Keri was

Employee of the Month. Gloria wondered if this was going to cost her – or rather Clegg – dearly.

But then, she reasoned, she could always say 'No!'

So she settled down with the tea and proceeded to happily look through inspiring brochures showing safaris in Africa, the Great Barrier Reef in Australia, amazing photos of exotic fish whilst snorkelling in the Maldives, Japan's cherry blossom season and all manner of incredible sights being offered to today's discerning travellers.

After a while she yawned, glanced at her empty teacup and said: 'Well that's all very lovely, ducks. But I don't have a passport no more, see. So we'd need to be looking at summat bit closer to home, love.'

Keri looked put out and her smile vanished. 'So where were you thinking of then?'

'Well I know people who've been on coach trips around the country. So let's have a look at some of them brochures. I've never been on a coach trip. Got any leaving some time soon – or even today, ducks?'

'Well no, madam! Of course not! You can't just come in here and expect to go on your holidays straight away, like that. Is that why you've brought your suitcase with you? Thinking you could just go off somewhere today?'

Gloria's tiny suitcase sat on the floor, looking quite curious in the travel shop. You never see people's suitcases in travel shops do you?

Suddenly thinking how ridiculous all this was Gloria burst

out laughing and then couldn't stop. 'Oh I'm a silly old woman, aren't I? I'm sorry, ducks. I wasn't really thinking straight!'

She had to get out of there as soon as. But she just couldn't stop laughing. It was infectious. The other two girls in the office started laughing too. She hoped they weren't laughing at her!

Just then one of the phones rang and a chap from out back came in to answer it.

Everyone started to pull themselves together.

'No! Really? Okay, then. Yes, yes. Well that's bloody incredible, Sam. No, they won't believe it!'

The girls glanced at each other, nervously. They probably weren't supposed to swear in front of the customers, no matter what the reason. Gloria looked at his badge: Dave. Dave seemed to be the only chap working there. He most likely got away with swearing because their boss was a bloke too.

He put the phone down and came over to Gloria.

'Right, missus. I overheard what you were sayin' just now and – guess what – this could be your lucky day! Well truth is, we've got a coach party leaving today for Eastbourne if you fancy going there. Two people have just cancelled so if you like you can take the place of one of 'em. We can do it for £150 for three nights, half board, instead of £180. It's yours if you want it. Tell me what to do. Sam's callin' me back in five.'

Gloria's mouth dropped open. Keri looked startled at this sudden amazing turn of events. *What on earth . . . ?* The other two girls jumped up.

'But where are they boarding from, Dave?' said one of them. 'Outside the bank, usually, round the corner, isn't it? Is that where they'll be today?'

'Yup. He'll be there in fifteen. Well, missus? You up for it?'

Well, what could Gloria say? She was still adventuring when she last looked. And yes, she actually DID fancy it!

'Why the hell not, lad? Yeah. Book me in, son. Go for it. Life's short. But can one of you show me where to go? And I'll be payin' by credit card, ducks!'

Chapter 25

Who'd've believed it?

'One moment, I'm seventy-nine years old, depressive and housebound, living in muck and surviving on potato soup and tea; the next, I'm travelling the nation and indulging in all manner of new experiences!' Gloria thought, delightedly.

Ooo! And this latest adventure wasn't even on her bucket list but she was going to add it immediately. Next stop for Gloria Frensham: Eastbourne!

She'd never been to Eastbourne before and didn't even know where it was. So the girls showed her on their map.

'It's on the south coast, right along from Southampton as you look at the map. See? There, look. And the sea's not murky like ours can be on the east coast. It's a turquoise like the photos in our window. Yes, really.'

And this was going to be a *proper* holiday. No more sleeping rough on floors, covered with newspapers like at Mabel's. No more taps seized up with no water or dodgy electricity like at her house. They were going to a proper three-star hotel, near the seafront, she was told. The price included breakfast and evening meal. So it was going to be much better value than the Norwich hotel.

The girls at the travel agent's all excitedly grabbed their coats and escorted Gloria down the road and around the corner to where the coach was collecting all the other punters, so they could wave her off. They were still giggling about the incredible turn of events that meant a seventy-nine-year-old lady had walked into their travel agent's, with her suitcase and within twenty-five minutes was off on her holidays! It was going to be party chatter, for them all, for years to come.

Everybody on the coach also smiled at her and waved from the back when she got on. They were a cheery lot.

'Hello, love!'

'– lo.'

'– lo.'

Gloria had to be helped up the steps by the driver. They were a bit steep, they were. She found a spare seat, next to an elderly gent. She secured her seat belt and then they shook hands and said hello.

It was a relief to be sitting down. It was so tiring running all over the place enjoying herself. Ha, ha! She was told it would be a three and a half hour trip, which would be just enough time for a nice little nap. She could hear the excited buzz of the other holiday-goers, as they organised themselves. It would be nice to meet some new people, she thought, as her eyelids closed, but socialising could wait.

* * *

Gloria awoke on the shoulder of the elderly man next to her, a couple of hours later. Oh! She'd been *mortified* by that.

'But you don't snore very loudly – or dribble,' he told her, with a smile, which made her more embarrassed than ever!

'Here, love. Glad you're awake. Where do you come from, then? My name's Dot,' said an old lady, behind her.

Gloria relished the chance to be interrupted by someone.

'Well my name's Gloria and I'm from Norwich actually. Where're you from?'

'Ely. My son dropped me off. Been going to Eastbourne every year since I was divorced. It's where I met my Stanley. He was me fourth husband, God rest 'is soul.'

'Fourth husband? Where'd you get the time to court and marry four men?' Gloria said, incredulous.

'Ha, ha. I always get asked that. I just loves going on nice honeymoons! No, just kidding! Ha, ha! Just kidding.'

'And my name is Joe,' said the elderly gentleman Gloria had fallen asleep on. He extended his hand for her to shake, again. She took it, blushing, feeling they were beyond hand-shakes now.

Then the coach erupted into a chorus of people asking after each other and the chatter went on, until the coach pulled up at their hotel, near the seafront.

The sun was shining and the sea was just as beautifully turquoise as Keri at the travel agency had said it would be. It even looked like photos she'd seen of the French Riviera!

Gloria was helped down the steps of the coach and stood

admiringly on the pavement. How *could* she be here in this beautiful place? She was smiling and felt totally happy. Two seagulls screeched overhead. She breathed in the warm salty air.

'Aaahh, lovely!'

Once they'd all left the coach and checked in, the receptionist told them they should meet in the bar, later that evening, for their welcome drink. At that time they'd also be informed about the hotel's facilities and any excursions planned for their stay, if they wished to partake.

'Oh, I've been to these things before, Gloria. Out to get a bit more cash outta ya. But sometimes the trips are good. I'm seein' some friends down here, so I won't be coming tonight but I'll see ya at meal times,' said one of the ladies.

'Is it worth me coming down for the meetin' then?' said Gloria, worriedly.

'Oh yes,' said Joe. 'They do different trips each year. Plus it's nice to meet everyone properly, you know. Come down about five-thirty. Dinner's at six-thirty. So I'll see you there later.'

'Cor, Tils, I'm gonna have a ball here,' Gloria said to her room, after checking in, and as she unpacked her few items and hung them in the wardrobe.

However, her bedroom here, she noted, was quite small. It was a single, unlike the one she'd stayed in at the Norwich hotel. But that didn't matter. Main thing was, it had a delightful sea view. 'Just like Mabel's got now,' she grinned, washing her smalls with bath gel provided, like she did at the Norwich hotel.

Afterwards she sat on a chair by the window, gazing out at a speedboat bouncing across the sparkling waves, sipping a nice cup of tea she'd made, from the complimentary refreshment tray. The boat sounded like a large wasp through the closed windows.

'Well, well. Eastbourne! Who'd've thought it?' she said, sighing in pleasure.

Chapter 26

Gloria sat between the two gents, Joe and Vittori, on the coach party's long dining table, in the hotel, that evening. The two men looked very smart in dark jackets and white shirts. Everybody had made an effort with their evening attire. Gloria couldn't remember the last time she'd worried about what to wear for an evening out.

The hotel's three-course meal plan meant you could start with prawn cocktail or vegetable soup followed by a chicken dinner or cheese salad and then trifle or fruit cocktail and tea or coffee.

She'd been told it was typical coach-party food, by Dot, implying it was somehow lacking. But Gloria didn't see it like that. Besides, she hadn't been used to any culinary delights in her life so far, so whatever had been served would have been perfectly fine. Plus she was amongst like-minded people in a lovely relaxing atmosphere. It was also nice that the waiters didn't rush them, between courses, and the diners even had time to chat with their servers, if they wished, which *was* definitely lacking in some places. So it made the whole event of 'eating dinner' a marvellous experience in Gloria's opinion.

Before dinner, at the five-thirty p.m. meeting, Gloria had chosen and paid for three excursions: the afternoon Eastbourne Bandstand concert, a city sightseeing tour and she was delighted that Joe, who seemed to be the perfect gentleman, had persuaded her to book the boat tour around Sovereign Harbour because she'd told him she'd never been on a boat before.

'Never been on a boat, Gloria? Goodness, then it's something you'll have to try while you're here. I'll come along too, of course, to show you the ropes, as it were, and what about you, Vittori? It's your favourite trip, isn't it?'

'Si. I like to do boating. It remind me of back when I was in Italy and my father, he had a boat and we went to fish because he have restaurant too. He dead now, so I no go back and my family here now.'

'Well, I think I'll try that then, gentlemen. Especially if you look after me on the boat. Otherwise, I don't think I'd have the guts to go.'

'You'll love it, Gloria, but you'll need to wear something warm because it can get rather chilly.'

'After the meal we usually have a walk along the prom, if you fancy doin' that, too, Gloria?' Dot called from further down the table. Dot wore a flowery Crimplene dress that looked as if it was two sizes too big for her. It reminded Gloria of the dresses she'd been given at Green's Nursing Home.

Gloria nodded and swallowed a mouthful of chicken. 'Not too far, I hope, but I fancy a little walk before bed.'

'Oh we usually have a drinkie poos after the walk, in the hotel bar, before we go to bed,' a lady called Freda told her. Freda looked quite elegant in a long white dress, trimmed with gold, and a grey shawl around her shoulders.

'And sometimes a game of cards too,' said someone else.

Gloria looked shocked. 'What? You do all that before bedtime? Are you all crackers?'

Everybody laughed and laughed.

'Nooooo. We just love to party. That's why we come here!' Freda said.

'We'll get you into it,' said a plump woman wearing a dark dress with a string of pearls round her neck. She'd introduced herself as Florence. 'But mebbe not if you're tired tonight. Are you tired, love?'

Gloria nodded. 'I am a bit. I've been havin' a rather tiring adventure this last week.'

'Ooo! The adventurous type. Well, go on then! Tell us all about it,' said Florence.

'You've got to tell us about your adventures now. We're a nosy lot and want to know what you've been up to!' said Freda, her eyes bright.

'Well, I'll finish me dinner first, if you don't mind, and then I'll tell you. And I'll tell youse, after me walk, in the bar with a glass of stout!'

* * *

153

She had them rolling with laughter at her exploits this last week, after escaping her dominating son. They were saddened by Mabel's problems but thought her daughter sounded hilarious with all her hang-ups.

'Aye. Wait 'til they get to our age. Then they'll realise what an UN-FUN time we have of it. Apart from excursions to Eastbourne, of course. That's when we get to let our hair down, not tear it out! Ha, ha!'

They said she should've brought her friends Jocelyn and Tilsbury with her and Gloria decided if there was a next time, she'd definitely bring them.

Gloria felt that the evening walk, along with the hum of easy-going chatter and lilting music coming from other cosily lit hotels and bars, had done her the world of good and she'd walked much further than she'd expected to. She was surprised at the still-salty atmosphere of the seaside, even at night. And, oh, it was just so lovely going out with that crazy fun-loving group of people she'd just met. The ease with which they gossiped and partied made her feel as though she'd been friends with them all her life.

Gloria had never had a crowd of friends like these. Even at school it had always just been her and Jocelyn and Mabel. In fact, she realised now that she'd felt isolated all her life, only knowing a few people. So she was loving the bonhomie of just being here with everyone else. It pepped her confidence up, no end, and she hadn't laughed so much, like this, since she was a girl.

And that was something else she'd realised.

One way or another, Gloria discovered, all the elderly people on the coach tour had experienced hardship, long-term health issues or their partners dying. But whatever their misfortunes, it was clear to see that this bunch of elderly people still looked forward to their uncertain futures – even *knowing* they were at the bottom of that proverbial hill. And they also looked forward to it with good humour and courage.

Joe told her that his wife had died four years ago. So his daughter had persuaded the distraught Joe to go away on a short break – she'd chosen Eastbourne for him – and it had brightened his heart and lifted his spirit so much that he'd been coming each year ever since.

'I never thought that meeting this crazy bunch of golden oldies would give me enough reason to pack my suitcase each year and come on holiday to Eastbourne. I wanted to die when my Carol died, you see. Couldn't see the point of life without her. She was my everything; my world. My daughter is sympathetic and helps me out, of course. She's very attentive and kind and she makes me go out and about a bit. She gets me to go to a Sudoku group and Bingo sometimes. But it's not the same as being with my Carol.'

Gloria had heard other stories like that.

'Putting one foot in front of the other is how I'd describe it,' Florence said. 'I lost both me parents and me husband to cancer of one sort or another, over an eight-month period. My son became me rock. Helped me no end, he did. And so I do this 'oliday twice a year now.'

'Twice?'

'Aye. Once in April, 'specially if it's been a rubbish winter. Then mid-summer 'cos it's the best time to visit. My treat to myself, love. You gotta have summat to look forward to, otherwise life gets unbearable, don't it?'

Gloria nodded with a sad smile.

She realised, at that moment, that everyone was very happy here. It was like a kind of 'time out' for old folks. But it was also a valuable, stimulating time away from all their problems; away from the problems that old age brings. It was also a welcome break away from overbearing or, sometimes equally frustrating, over-caring family members.

Everyone was happy and relaxed, here, and in the mood for having fun. So it was a nurturing environment to be included in.

Gloria smiled at them all. 'You're an inspiring bunch, I must say. And it's a real pleasure to know you all,' she said quietly.

'Aw, that's a nice thing to say!' said Freda.

'Oh, how lovely you are to say that,' said Florence.

They all bunched around her and rubbed her arm or hugged her. Vittori took her hand and kissed it and Joe kissed her cheek. She blushed and everyone started laughing.

'*Joseph's got a girlfriend. Joseph's got a girlfriend . . .*'

Chapter 27

The next day Gloria put on another of her new dresses, a three-quarter-sleeved cherry pink floral dress with a pale blue background – the perfect dress, she'd decided, for summer holidays – in order to spend what could potentially be an exciting morning boating, with Joe and Vittori.

It was still sunny but the wind had risen to a force three, which meant their tour boat in the harbour wallowed around more than it would have done if they'd taken the excursion the day before.

Gloria admitted she felt a bit seasick and Vittori told her not to look down at her feet but to concentrate on the harbour views of boats and yachts. Seagulls glided above them in the warm air currents.

Joe sat next to her, his arm linked through hers, with Vittori sitting opposite. The boat lurched in places, especially when another boat went past, a feeling Gloria didn't like. The person steering reeled off a commentary, telling them how relatively new the harbour was and yet how much life it encouraged to the area, by way of shops, restaurants, sailing businesses and tourists.

When the boat docked they clambered off and found a nearby café for a cuppa. Gloria was glad she'd taken her jacket and scarf because Joe was right. It had been chillier than she'd expected.

'Warmed up now?' said Joe.

Gloria nodded. 'I feel better than I did. Didn't expect to have an upset tummy, though, going boatin'.'

'Sometimes it happen,' said Vittori solemnly, drinking his espresso. Gloria could see he'd once been a very handsome man. She'd even noticed Florence giving him the eye across the table last night! He wore a dark green polo shirt with a light jacket and smoked Gauloises French cigarettes.

'But did you enjoy the experience?' said Joe.

'I've had a lovely morning, thanks to you both helping me with everything. So yes. Ooh look, they sell postcards here. Might buy a couple and send 'em home.'

They joined Florence, Freda and Dot on the afternoon trip to the brass band concert at Eastbourne Bandstand. Most of the other coach party travellers had seen it before and went for a walk down the pier, or met up with friends and family, instead. Gloria sat in the sunshine, thoroughly enjoying the lively familiar music and heartily joining in when people were singing or clapping along with the tunes.

'Do you fancy a little dance with me, Gloria?' said Joe. 'This song *Chanson d'Amour* is my favourite tune.'

'We can't do that here, Joe, I'm sure.'

'They won't mind! Besides they'll think we're a couple of

old fogies who've lost their marbles! It's handy being old sometimes.'

'Go for it, Gloria!' Freda encouraged.

Gloria grinned. 'Ha, ha. Okay. All right. Come on then.'

He stood up and helped Gloria to her feet and they moved away from the seating area. Gloria hadn't danced in years. Joe looked very smart, today, in his dark blue jacket. He was a true gent, Gloria realised. He put his arm round her waist and they just danced side to side in time with the music. Gloria couldn't stop smiling. It felt lovely and took her back to the tea dances she used to go to, with Arthur. People in the audience were smiling at them, too; no one was being unkind or tutting.

She realised she'd never experienced the kind of joyful fun she was discovering on this impromptu holiday with her new-found friends. No wonder some of them kept coming back year after year. It was truly marvellous. Although, that day on the beach near Sheringham with Tilsbury, Gloria thought with a smile, had come a keen second.

The next day Gloria awoke and stretched. She had to keep pinching herself to be reminded that she was actually here, in Eastbourne, with the sea and beach right there, across the road, beyond her bedroom window. She made herself a cup of tea and tidied her room. She didn't like the idea of the chambermaid coming in and finding her living the way she used to live.

She'd made a promise to Green's Nursing Home as well as

to herself *twice* that she would never hoard or be messy ever again and was reasonably confident she'd keep that promise. She'd seen first-hand how disruptive it was to people's lives, especially hers and Mabel's.

Gloria knew the sightseeing tour on the green and cream Eastbourne buses was going to be great. Joe came with her and Dot and her friends were there and Florence came too. Vittori's granddaughter had come to take him back to her house for the day, since she lived nearby. A few of the other coach party holidaymakers had family members in East Sussex and visited them while they were down here, too.

'Um, if you don't mind, I don't wanna get off the bus just yet, Joe. I'd just like to sit here and watch the world pass by and see everythin' once and then mebbe get off the next time round, when I see somewhere I fancy goin'.'

And so that's what they did. The other ladies got off and on at the various attractions Eastbourne had to offer but Joe stayed on the bus with Gloria, seeing as it was her first time here. They got off at Beachy Head to take in the air or rather nearly get swept away since the wind had picked up by the middle of the day.

'I know, Joe! Let's pop into that pub over there for a spot of lunch. My treat for you showin' me the sights!'

'Oh! Are you sure? Well that would be nice, Gloria. Thank you.'

The ambience of the pub was very welcoming with its idle chatter, clinking glasses and a warm, traditional feel in the décor. They chose a table indoors and ordered fish and chips and a glass of lager each. Gloria squeezed mayonnaise over her fish when it arrived and they, mainly, ate in silence.

'You see, this is what I miss with my wife Carol. We used to go to those tea dances and we often had a couple of holidays a year to different places,' said Joe as he put his knife and fork together, afterwards.

'But you like Eastbourne now.'

'I really enjoy it, Gloria. You get to meet so many nice people – like yourself, of course. You remind me a bit of my Carol. She liked trying new things. She was a courageous sort. But she – um – she got leukaemia.'

As Joe's gaze fell, Gloria reached across the table and held his hand.

'Oh dear, that's sad, Joe. Life's very hard, I know. But we have to go on, don't we? We have to be positive in our outlook. That's what I've learnt from all youse anyway. And your Carol would've wanted you to go on, too. She'd've still wanted you to have some happy times, Joe, even though she's not actually here with you. D'you remember that programme called *Waiting for God*? That actress, what was her name – oh yes – Stephanie Cole. She was hilarious, wasn't she? So funny. I loved it. She was always lamenting about life, wasn't she? But I can see that you've got to lift yer head towards the sun and keep fightin' for life.'

Joe nodded. 'You're right. But it's difficult sometimes. And when it's difficult, I sometimes um – *I shouldn't be telling you all this*,' he said, tears forming at the edges of his eyes.

'It's all right, Joe. I know what you mean. You really don't feel like goin' on sometimes, do you? It's like there's no point when you can't be with yer wife or husband who's passed. And our families nag us to keep going, don't they? They keep telling us we've got to carry on trying to find meaningful stuff to do, even though we might only have a few months or a few years left. But it still feels pointless, doesn't it? Because we're only really just waitin' to join them, aren't we? We just want to be with them. Our loved ones. Just like that *Waiting for God* programme really.'

Joe nodded, vigorously, sniffing. 'That's exactly it, Gloria.'

Gloria sighed deeply. 'I know and, truth be told, Joe, back when I was depressed, I used to think that I couldn't wait for my Big Sleep either. You see, I was very lonely after me adoptive mum, Alice, died 'cos I didn't have any other family at the time, apart from Arthur and our son, Clegg. But when my lovely Arthur died I really started hoarding things. I guess I was locking myself away from the world and what I thought might be more misery. But since them days – and that's not so long ago now – since then, I've been feeling a bit more upbeat about things because I got some help from a social worker called Kate at a nursing home I stayed in for a while. And now, well, I've been havin' so many weird, amazing adventures that I think I actually *want* to go on a bit longer.

'It's like I've just woken up from a long sleep and realised there's lots of other things I still want to do. I probably even missed out on loads of things when I was living with my

Arthur 'cos we didn't really do much together except raise Clegg. So I'm curious to keep going and find out what else is round the next corner. I mean, I've no idea what's next for me, either, Joe, but . . . well, I'm just curious to find out. While I've still got the chance to, you see. And that's a chance that my Arthur and your Carol don't have any more. So we're quite fortunate, in that respect, when you thinks about it, aren't we?'

Joe nodded but Gloria could see he looked glum. So she put her arms round him and held him a while. She felt him relax into her and then sensed he was about to start sobbing, when his body suddenly heaved. Ah, poor Joe. Men cry too. She knew that.

'It's okay, Joe. Let it out. C'mon let's go outside and you can have a moment. I still get them too, you know. So don't worry. I won't be tellin' anyone.'

Tears streaked his face. 'But I miss her so much. Always have.'

'Course you do, ducks. They're in our hearts. My Arthur is too. I sometimes cry myself to sleep, thinking about him. I think everybody does that, Joe. There, there. C'mon now. Look, let's get the bus back and then you go have a lie-down before dinner. We're back home tomorrow, anyways.'

Chapter 28

The last night of her Eastbourne adventure had Gloria singing at the top of her voice with everybody else at the dinner table; glasses of sparkling wine clinking, toasting the wonderful time they'd all had, new friends made and even Joe had recovered and was joining in enthusiastically. Phone numbers and addresses were swapped. Gloria had given Clegg's details, not completely sure where her fortunes would take her next.

After dinner, Joe caught up with Gloria in reception as she was making her way back to her room.

'Thanks for listening, Gloria,' he whispered, looking around him, making sure no one was watching. He then placed a small gift into her hand. 'But please open this later.'

They all had sore heads the next day at breakfast and by the time they'd climbed back onto their coach, most had fallen asleep before the coach hit the A11.

Gloria got dropped off around the corner from the travel agency where she'd booked her holiday, a mere few days ago. Everyone was saying goodbye and hugging her and talking about meeting up same time, same place next year.

'That's if we're still alive then, hey, Gloria?!' they giggled, as they were being collected by their respective families and friends.

Joe had already kissed her goodbye and left with his daughter, after introducing her to Gloria. But because Gloria wasn't being picked up by anyone, she was finally left standing on the pavement, quite alone with just her tiny suitcase and a bag of gifts for company. She let out a mournful sigh.

She always felt downhearted once she'd experienced something powerful or enjoyed something wonderful. Euphoria, she noted, never endured. There was always a 'coming down' period afterwards. Ying and yang. Hot and cold. Happy and (too much) sad.

She hoped Joe would be all right. He lived with his daughter now so at least he had some company. It was certainly better than going back to an empty house like she knew Florence would have to do. But perhaps Florence liked living on her own.

'Wonder where I'll end up?' she said out loud and felt in her pocket for a handkerchief to wipe away the tears of self-pity starting to drip down her cheeks.

Her hand closed around the tiny gift Joe had given her. She took it out, placed her suitcase and the gifts on the pavement and opened the prettily wrapped present.

It was a locket. It looked to be nine-carat gold, no less. Gloria gasped.

And inside was a tiny picture, that Joe must've got from somewhere, maybe off a brochure, of the bandstand at Eastbourne where she'd danced with him . . .

And then Gloria really did burst into tears, standing on that pavement as people scurried around her heading off in all sorts of directions to who-knows-or-cares where, as huge blobs of salty tears washed over her.

* * *

'Thanks for coming to get me, Joss,' said Gloria, as she wriggled out of Jocelyn's clapped-out Mini, at the gate of her friend's council house.

They were greeted by six howling rescue cats swirling round their ankles at the door. It was obviously feeding time. There were two tabbies, three ginger toms and one pregnant black and white cat – all in varying degrees of neglect. Inside her house were three adorable black and white kittens.

'I see you've narrowed them down a bit since last time. You had near on twenty at one time, didn't you? Are you still rescuing them?'

Jocelyn nodded. 'I am, for me sins. Can't help myself, Glor. I know they make a mess and too much noise, half the time. And I know it's what sent Tils out me door. But I feel so sorry for them when people are rotten to 'em. I've rehomed a few. I work with the Cat Protection people on that score. But I lost two last year. Got squashed by maniacs speedin' round these estates. Sad, really. Anyways. Here, Marv. Look what Gloria got us.'

Jocelyn was thrilled to receive a carrier bag of goodies that Gloria had got for her and Marvin from Eastbourne. There was a bottle of wine, a bottle of cider, some chocolates, two mugs and a couple of tea towels with a printed picture of Beachy Head on them.

'We ain't got yer postcard yet, love. But thanks for these anyway.'

'You're welcome, ducks. So, seen anythin' of Tilsbury, lately?'

Jocelyn bent down and picked up one of the kittens. 'Nah. He still keeps poking around when we're out but we haven't seen him in a while now. Could be anywhere.'

'Joss, why d'you put up with his nicking? I've always wondered that.'

Jocelyn shrugged, stroking the cute kitten. 'Dunno really. Well we all goes back a long way, don't we, and Marvin feels a bit sorry for him too on account he's got nowt. Well, he has his state pension. It comes here. All his mail comes here, in fact. But he's got nowhere proper to live, has he? Actually, love, he went to the council when we got back from Sheringham. They sent him to social services. He was hoping to get a flat or council house or summat. But they said he'd have to find somewhere himself that he can pay for, out his pension, because they only accommodate certain categories of people nowadays, like one-parent families and whatnot. Plus they got a long list of folk with special problems, needin' assistance, before him. So he'd be at the bottom of that list. He asked how long it'd take before he got to the top of the list and they said it could be years.'

Yes, Gloria had heard it wasn't as easy to get help from the social, as some people thought. She felt sorry for Tilsbury because since Clegg had kicked him out of her house there really was nowhere else for him to go. So unless social services helped him out with something regular, he was stuck.

But Gloria was thrilled Jocelyn had asked if she'd like to stay at their place, for a few days, as long as she could tolerate the cats, before she went back to Clegg and Val's.

'To acclimatise before the shit hits the fan, as it were, love?' Jocelyn had said with a grin.

Well, yes.

That was a most welcome idea because at that moment, Gloria had one or two more things to sort out before she tackled her errant son and his wife.

Chapter 29

Gloria was pleased Jocelyn could drop her off early so she could spy on Clegg and Val to make sure they went to work. She had no intention of walking straight into a row. But, oh joy! She could see that the children were back home, judging by the activity in Clegg's driveway. And she would've *loved* to have walked straight over and hugged them and told them all about her adventures and learned about theirs. All that, though, would have to wait for another time. There were other more pressing things she needed to do before that.

Gloria intended to try and find out exactly what Clegg was doing with her house before they came home, later that day, so there'd be no more surprises when she finally got to talk to them both.

Jocelyn had said the For Sale boards were still outside her house and that there'd been comings and goings – viewings – according to nosy Mrs Daly. But there were no SOLD boards up yet.

Gloria saw a young man she presumed was Adam leave in a car with some friends. Jessie was the last to walk out of the house at 8.55 a.m. They both looked very different now. They'd shot out in all directions. Adam had a large frame like his dad and Jessie was petite, like Val but with long dark hair. Gloria was thrilled at the sight of her wonderful grandchildren, after all these years. Ah well. One day soon they'd have a lovely reunion. But it wouldn't be just yet.

Gloria still had her key and as soon as the coast was clear she eased herself out from the hedge she was hiding behind and let herself into Clegg's home. She didn't like standing for long periods of time at seventy-nine. It had been very uncomfortable hiding behind that hedge just so she could do her bit of sleuthing. She'd got a couple of odd stares, too, from curious dog walkers.

She also needed a bath because Jocelyn's shower wasn't working properly at the moment and after the luxurious hotel baths she'd had of late, she knew she couldn't settle for a cold dribble. But first she went into the kitchen and rooted around in the kitchen drawers, where she knew they kept their day-to-day paperwork.

It didn't take long for her to lay her hands on what she was looking for – three sets of particulars for her house. But – best of all – *there* was her photo album, in the same drawer! She took it out and hugged it. It even smelt the same. She had a quick look inside. No, nothing had been removed. It was all there. Even the photo of her birth mum and dad on their wedding day. Phew! What a relief! She didn't know *what* she'd have done if Clegg had thoughtlessly DUMPED that!

She put the album down, for a moment, and looked at her

housing particulars. No, that couldn't be right, she thought, flicking through it. Oh my God! The estate agents were selling her house for . . .

'Good grief – £385,000 with one estate agent, carpets of your choice included in the price – God, £9,000 for carpets? What a rip-off! Surely it wouldn't cost that much to put new carpets in throughout? And £375,000 with the other two agents but no carpet deal. But that's a bloody *fortune*! Is my little house *really* worth that much? Oh my God!'

Gloria was so shocked she had to sit down.

She couldn't stop staring at the typed details and photos of the house she no longer recognised without its familiar clutter in every room, on every surface. Jocelyn was right. It had been coated in white paint throughout, which made it look spacious and, maybe, fresh but it also looked very stark. It was certainly no longer her house. The outside had even been 'landscaped' according to the typed details. And there was now a slabbed 'car port' in place of the shed that used to house all her mum's old stuff. What a ruddy amazing transformation! Gloria couldn't believe it.

After a while she rose gloomily and switched the kettle on for a cuppa, because she realised she belonged nowhere now. Her house was no longer her house. And there was certainly nothing homely staring out at her from the pages of the estate agent's details. She wasn't quite sure what Clegg and Val had in mind for her but she knew it wasn't going to be anything rosy. Regrettably, after all the carefree fun she'd been having, flying around the nation, these housing particulars had brought her back down to earth with a ruddy great hard bump.

She ignored the whistling kettle as she walked down the corridor, deep in thought, to her bedroom. The bed had been made and it was clean and tidy but it looked as if she'd never been there. It was, in fact, as stark as the estate agent's particulars. There was also nothing homely, she realised, about Clegg and Val's home, either, apart from their lovely garden.

But maybe they'd moved her out already? Maybe – oh no – maybe an old people's home was now waiting for her, far away from everyone she knew.

It was totally disheartening.

She ran a bath, stripped and when she'd got the right depth and temperature she climbed carefully in, lowering herself with some difficulty, onto her knees and then getting her legs out straight, once she'd sat down. She lay down in the soapy gel suds with a wheeze. She actually found it easier getting out than in. But she'd needed that bath. She loved having baths now.

Before being rescued she hadn't had one in years and years, with all the problems in her old house. She'd had baths in the three hotels she'd recently stayed in, though. She preferred them to being seated on a plastic chair in the showers they insisted you use in old people's homes, with high-powered water peppering down on your head – even though baths were hard to negotiate. One day she'd have to succumb to showers only; she knew that much. But for now, she was enjoying this – possibly her last bath.

She lay there, after she'd washed, until the water began to turn cool. Then she sat up, managed to get into a kneeling position, again, and tentatively got out, holding on to the edge of the bath – there was no grab rail – and dried off. She felt so tired. She also felt a little apprehensive. What were her rights in all of this? Well she knew one thing, for sure. The house was *hers* not Cleggy's. He couldn't sell something that didn't belong to him. But where were her documents – the deeds to her house? She needed them but they weren't in the kitchen.

Clegg had dealt with everything after Arthur died.

Gloria had spent long hours grieving her lovely Arthur, back then, not wanting to see anyone or do anything. She'd been very depressed. But Cleggy had looked after her, popping round after work when he first started in his job, straight out of the army, as a security guard. He'd fed her and taken control of every situation she could no longer deal with. Plus he didn't mention her 'collections' of stuff, as she called her hoarding back then. So it was fine, when she didn't know or care what she was doing, in respect of her grief and her hoarding woes. So, admittedly, yes! Clegg *had* helped her in those days.

But now, she realised, she wanted some control back over her life as well as access to her 'assets', as Jocelyn had informed her that her house would now be referred to.

She didn't know where to start or how to deal with reining

in her son's attitude now he'd changed. And he'd certainly changed. He'd always been quite cocky as a teenager and often brought trouble to their door but he'd stepped up when she was grief-stricken about Arthur. Yet, nowadays, he was morose and had little patience with her. Somewhere along the line, something had changed with him but she didn't know what had caused that to happen and why. Yet if they were to carry on as mother and son, in some context, they needed to reach an agreement about what was to be done with everything, including the sale of her house.

She dressed again and walked back into the kitchen and flicked the kettle switch on, so she could make some tea and have a sandwich before she went out again.

In the lounge she spied her London postcard sitting on the mantelpiece above the hearth. Well at least they hadn't thrown it out in disgust. Maybe there was hope. Or maybe it meant nothing. The Eastbourne one was nowhere to be seen. Perhaps it hadn't arrived yet.

But she realised if Clegg wanted to play dirty she would simply have to go and see a solicitor and sort everything out properly. She didn't want to do that. It felt mean, even though he'd treated her badly. But he'd caused this unpleasantness and so now she had to deal with it. Trying to talk sensibly with him wouldn't work because he always managed to turn things around so it looked as though *she* was somehow in the wrong. And she couldn't take that any more. She couldn't stand being put down by him all the time.

It had to stop.

Jocelyn had told her about a cheapish solicitor, called Ron Byrd, who was a one-man band. Jocelyn had used him when she and Tilsbury divorced. So, if he was still in business, perhaps he'd give Gloria some free advice and even if she had to pay for it, well then, she still had the credit card Clegg had given her, after all.

Chapter 30

Gloria got the bus into town because she knew Jocelyn and Marvin were betting at the dog track today. They'd left a written message on their hall table for Tilsbury to let him know that, whether he sneaked back in to annoy them, or to pick up his mail, Gloria was back and wanted to see him.

She found out where Ron Byrd's office was, so she went to see him. As she stepped off the bus she took a deep breath. This was all starting to seem a bit real now. What a shame they couldn't all sit down like adults and discuss what was to be done with her house.

Ron Byrd's office was on the first floor of a block of offices. The lift was out of order so the flight of stairs had her gasping and wheezing for breath. As she approached the reception desk, panting, the receptionist said Ron wouldn't be able to see her because he was tied up with client meetings all day and that she'd have to make an appointment for another day if she wanted to see him.

'Oh Ron Byrd's come up in the world now has he? He never had anyone mindin' him before!' Gloria said exasperated, as she looked around at the tired reception area with drooping spider plants and scratched faux leather seats – or were they meant to look like that? She perched on the edge of one. 'Plus I've just climbed all the way up those ruddy stairs, love. Would be better if you'd mended the lift, wouldn't it?'

'We need a new lift, actually, ma'am. But the other folks in this building ain't got the money to pay for a new one and the landlord says he don't want to pay for one either. So it's a tricky situation. Anyway I'm Ron's receptionist as well as his secretary, so I do everything except speak to clients. And I'm in charge of his diary and he's busy all day.'

'Oh that's nice. Well, love, I have to say that I've just about had a skinful of late and, if he's to be my solicitor then I want a few quick words with him as soon as.'

'Yes, well, like I say he's busy at the moment. I'll look at the diary and then we'll find you a spot.'

At that moment there was a roar from the office behind the girl.

'Oh he's in with clients is he? Well I don't think he'd be roarin' like a lion if there was clients in with him, lass!'

Gloria got up.

'Er well no! No but yes! He's seeing clients in about five minutes you see. So you'd have to wait anyway –'

'Well I'm not waitin', lass. I'm goin' in.'

And with that Gloria strode purposely behind the reception desk, knocked on Ron Byrd's door and entered his office.

Ron Byrd was a stout man who clearly chain-smoked,

judging by the overflowing ashtray on his desk. And it seemed he was happy to work with – ahem – unruly piles of paperwork covering his desk. Gloria raised her eyebrows at that. Living in chaos was one thing but how was anyone able to work, professionally, in that sort of environment? A wooden frame with his credentials hung slightly crookedly on his wall.

'Okay, well,' she began. 'Right now, I know I ain't got an appointment but I'll be quick. Do you remember Jocelyn Harrington or you'd'a known her as Jocelyn Hunter when she was married? Well, anyway she recommended you and all I want, at this stage, is for you to answer me a few quick questions.'

Ron Byrd roared again but it wasn't actually a roar. He clearly had a very bad cold and that roar was the sound of a huge sneeze. He had a large white handkerchief to catch it.

'Bless you, love,' said Gloria.

Ron Byrd shifted in his seat. 'Thank you. Right, now, who d'you say? Jocelyn? Nope. Don't hear the name Jocelyn bandied about much these days, do you? Oh, wait a minute! Yeah! I remember. Loud mouth. Argumentative sort,' Ron Byrd said, screwing his face up in an unpleasant way. 'So. You related?'

'No, she's my friend. Now the girl outside says you've got another appointment in five minutes so I'll be quick. I've got a house in my name that my son is tryin' to sell from under me. First, can he do that and second he's hidden me documents provin' it's mine. Can I get him to give 'em back?'

'Right, well that'll be a No to the first question and a Yes to the second.'

'Ah well that's encouragin'. So could I tell him you're going to be my solicitor if he starts gettin' stroppy with me? And how much do ya charge?'

'Yes you can tell anybody I'm your solicitor. I need all the business I can get these days! And my charges vary depending what's involved. Debs, the girl outside, will give you a sheet with my charges on or we can have a chat about what we'll be doing and I can give you a quote.'

'Right, well I think first off I'll just *say* you're me solicitor and then take it from there, if ya don't mind. Can you give me a card to rub under his nose?'

Ron Byrd sniggered. 'Sure. Pick one up off the front desk.'

'Well thank you very much, Ron Byrd. You're a good 'un.'

'But you haven't seen my charges yet.'

Chapter 31

Gloria felt mountains better, after her little chat with Ron Byrd. And having Ron's business card now meant that she, too, could do 'business' with Clegg and Val. It wasn't quite war but it certainly meant she was a force to be reckoned with.

Plus, knowing she could get help with her quest – if she needed to – was a bargaining tool, if nothing else. She'd done her homework. And it had given her bags of confidence, knowing she was about to take back some of the control over her life.

Gloria had known for quite a while that she simply couldn't allow Clegg to continue treating her as though she was a stupid imbecile. She needed him to respect her, the way he should, as his mother. She also knew that it would be hard for her to force this issue with him. Perhaps that's why she'd allowed him to treat her the way he had, all these years. Because it was easier than fighting all the time. But it hadn't helped anyone – least of all her. So she knew it was going to be difficult to be firm with him; to put him in his place. But she also knew she had to stick to her guns. For all their sakes.

After leaving Ron's she walked into a bank, around the corner from the solicitor's office, and opened an account with £100 of Clegg's money that she'd taken out of the hole-in-the-wall in Sheringham. She gave her own home address, not Clegg's, in case things suddenly changed and the house wasn't sold, for some reason. And Gloria showed the teller a recent utility bill of hers, that Jocelyn told her she'd need, as well as an old library card with a faded photo, for identification. She'd found both in Clegg's kitchen drawer.

She'd had to answer quite a few questions about herself before the bank account could be opened. In the past, Arthur had done this type of thing for her and then Clegg had taken over dealing with her paperwork once his dad had passed. After the bank, she found a little café and treated herself to a well-earned cup of tea and a pink iced bun before picking up some fish and chips and then heading back to Jocelyn's on the bus.

When she got back she was pleased to see Tilsbury was there, having a cup of tea with Jocelyn and Marvin. They hugged for a while.

'Get a room, bruv!' snorted Marvin, with a grin.

Gloria chose to ignore him. 'Oh I've missed ya, Tils.'

'Me too,' said Tilsbury. 'So c'mon tell me all about yer adventures.'

'Well, first we'll have these fish and chips I've bought us all and then we'll have a little natter, ducks. Plus, can I make a couple of phone calls, Joss? I can pay ya if ya like.'

'Nah, what's the cost of a couple of phone calls, love. You brought us dinner. Dial away to yer heart's content.'

* * *

The next day at 7.45 a.m., Clegg, Val, Adam and Jessie were settling down to their breakfast of cornflakes, tea and toast when they were startled by a loud banging on their front door.

'What the – ?' began Clegg, annoyed, mug of tea in hand.

Adam got there first, sliding down the hall in his socks. He opened the door cautiously and there was Gloria's face, beaming at him.

'Hello, Adam love! My how you've grown! Crikey you're almost as tall as my Cleggy! Don't remember me do you, love? I'm your gran. Yer dad's mum!'

'Oh hi, Gran; Dad said you were stayin'. Well he said you'd gone off. Swore a bit he did. You've been to London. Cool place ain't it?'

He moved forward to hug Gloria.

''Tis that, love. Especially Big Ben.'

'Who is it, Adam? Who's at the bloody door, at this hour?' Clegg bellowed, finishing his swig of tea.

Val walked into the hall. 'Gloria! Where the hell've you been? We've been worried sick!'

She didn't move to hug Gloria.

'Cleggy's been going off his rocker,' she said in a flat tone.

Gloria regarded her stiffly. 'Well I didn't think you wanted me back, with all the arguments and tippy-toeing around me. I don't like all that unpleasantness, love.'

Adam looked puzzled but went back to finish his breakfast. *Adults*, his expression clearly said.

Clegg appeared at the door, the rage bright red on his face. 'Well, Mother, I think we need to have a talk.'

Gloria always felt wobbly, dealing with him. He had a certain knack of always making her feel foolish. But, today, she moved towards the lounge, ahead of him – admittedly, with more certainty than she felt. But she was determined. It had to be done. Val followed.

'You two get yourselves off. See youse later, guys,' she shouted to her children and then closed the lounge door for privacy.

Clegg sat on the sofa, his arms crossed, a grim expression on his face. 'So what've you got to say for yourself, then, Mother?'

Gloria sat on the edge of the armchair opposite and also steeled herself, arms folded.

Wasn't he supposed to jump up and hug her, now she'd come back from God knows where, knowing that here she was safe and sound and back home, where she belonged?

But although she felt threatened by Cleggy's unfriendly manner, she didn't like the thought of what she needed to say to him and Val. Not one little bit.

Chapter 32

'I am your mother, Cleggy. And let me tell you, you have no right to talk to me as though I was summat nasty you'd stepped in.'

Clegg shifted in his seat.

'You and Val have been controlling me for a long time now. And I will admit that I didn't realise it until I spoke to those lovely people at the nursin' home. Fact, I couldn't believe I'd let things get so outta hand that I really didn't know what I was doin' any more.'

Nobody spoke.

'I was depressed. But what did you care? You left me to rot in my rotten house. I was probably in need of some mental health attention too. But no. You were happy to see me deteriorating like that, weren't you, Cleggy? Because that way you could tell everyone I was a hopeless case and then, once you got your hands on my money, you could put me away somewhere, far away from you all. In fact, I think by getting me put away you saw it as one less problem for you to have to deal with. And I think you do see me as a "problem". *Not*, unfortunately, as yer mother, son.'

'It's not like that,' Val retorted.

'Where the *hell* have you been, Mother?' Clegg said through clenched teeth.

'I've been away on my holidays and to – hmm, what's that expression – oh yes, to *find* myself.'

'Oh yes? And where did you find yourself?'

Gloria shrugged. 'Here and there, actually. Well, all over the place really. I've learned a lot from my travels.'

'Have you now? And did you enjoy using all my money whilst you were doing that?'

'You kept giving me credit cards, when yer dad died and I never spent one single penny on them. Until now. Plus you never told me what I COULDN'T spend it on!'

'True.' Val smiled.

'This is not a fucking joke, Val!'

Val sighed and folded her arms.

Just then the door flew open and Jessie popped her head in. 'Grandma! Adam said you were here at last! Oh I've missed you!'

'I've missed you too, my darling. Oh you've changed so much. Both of you've changed.'

Jessie bundled in and threw herself onto Gloria. She smelled of something sweet, like fruit. They both hugged long and hard. Clegg and Val exchanged nervous glances.

'Okay, Jessie. We're talking to Grandma. You can see her later. Don't be late for Ben and close the door on your way out,' said Val, in a faux friendly way.

'Okay, Gran. Catch up later. Byeee.'

'Bye, darling.'

After the door closed, Clegg said through clenched teeth, 'Of course you won't have access to your grandchildren if we have to move you into a home for your own good. You do see that, Mother, don't you . . . ?'

Gloria tensed, sadly realising Tilsbury's prophecy about her being carted off to an old people's home in another town could well be true. But she'd had enough of all this crap and drama. She hadn't brought Clegg up to act like a spoiled brat or treat her atrociously. How did people change like that? She stood up because her back was aching.

'Well you've never given me access to them before, so why would you give me access to them now? But it's all part of your plan, isn't it?' she said pointing a finger. 'Oh yes, Cleggy. I can see the whole picture now! Get me certified and then admitted somewhere. That way someone else foots the bill and YOU can go off into the sunset with my money. Or so you think. But you can't, you know.'

She paused to catch her breath.

All this was making her tired. She shouldn't have to fight her son like this. He shouldn't have put them all in this awful position where she was having to fight for a right to be heard; a right to be cared for; her right to be loved by someone . . .

'Anyway, for your information. I've been to see a solicitor –'

'You've WHAT, Mother?' Clegg nearly yelled.

'Yes, this's his business card here,' she said wagging it in front of him. 'I've told him all about you – about the situation – and he says I've got a case.'

'For fuck's sake, you stupid old bat! After everything I've done for you? I looked after you when Dad died. I bring you stuff all the time. Who do you think you are, all of a sudden?'

Val jumped up. 'Clegg! Don't speak to your mother like that! All this is getting out of hand. It's not right. But *she's* right. You can't sell her house without her say-so.'

'No, actually, Val. It's all right. I *want* him to sell my house now!'

* * *

Clegg's jaw dropped and he looked properly astonished, which made Gloria chuckle inwardly. *That* had stopped him in his tracks!

'What do you mean, you *want* me to sell the house?' he said slowly.

'It needs selling. It's far too big for me now and I no longer want to live there. I must say I was bloody annoyed when I found out what you intended to do with it from Jocelyn via Mrs Daly but I've been away, as you know. And now – well – I've changed me mind about wanting to keep it. Have you had any offers on it yet? You're asking a good price for it! Where'd you get a figure like that from?'

Clegg and Val exchanged certain looks, which Gloria read

190

as, *how does she know what price it's selling for*? She liked that they felt put out by her ingenuity.

'Oh and just to let you know,' Gloria continued, her confidence soaring, as her words scored the desired effect, 'I've got a new bank account now. Sorted that out yesterday. So when we get the right person, I'll just sign on the dotted line and get the solicitor to wire the money direct to me at my new bank account. You can do what you like with my old one.'

Clegg actually began to splutter, as though he couldn't get his words out. Val's mouth opened in shock. But she was the first to recover.

'Well, good for you, Gloria. You've grown balls since you were away. Shame Cleggy hasn't got any!' she said and turned and marched out of the lounge.

Chapter 33

Gloria Frensham finally had a plan.

So she let everyone who needed to know where she was moving to. It was only for a little while, she said, whilst everything got sorted out.

She'd asked Jocelyn to drive her back to the hotel at Sheringham and bartered for an agreeable price so she could stay in a single room for a couple of weeks or so. It was far enough away from Clegg and Val; although Adam and Jessie did take it in turns to drive over to meet her and get to know her again, without Cleggy being there, dampening everyone's spirits. Plus now she had her own breathing space it meant she could simply walk along the edge of the sea and reminisce and grieve openly, if she wished.

Yes, *grieve*.

The main reason she'd moved away was that Clegg had forgotten to tell her a vital piece of news: her dear friend Mabel had died. Well, that was the icing on the cake for Gloria, with her son. If he'd been a normal genial person he could have let her know about her friend's demise the day she called to see her family, instead of bellowing at her the moment she stepped into the house. It was Val who'd actually rung Gloria, at Jocelyn's, to pass on the message.

Apparently, poor Mabel had died the week following their phone call, when she'd been gleefully telling Gloria that everything was grand, now she'd moved in with her son. Her tummy pains had turned out to be bowel cancer. So her appointment with the doctor had seen her rushed into hospital for an emergency operation but she'd died there, a few days later. Gloria didn't know all the details. But fortunately David and Sandie had been at her side. She hadn't died alone, at least.

Jocelyn kindly offered to drive Gloria back up to Skegness for the funeral.

'Oh thank you, Joss. But it's miles away! Will yer little car make it?'

'Well, it will now, love. We just got it serviced. So it should run all right. Plus she was my mate too ya know and I've never been to Skeggy.'

Although she was nervous about whether Jocelyn's car would actually survive the hundred or so miles each way, Gloria finally agreed: 'Providing you let me pay you petrol money – and NO arguing about that!'

So the two of them drove up to Skegness to give Mabel a good send-off. It was just a small gathering consisting of family and Gloria and Jocelyn. They stood side by side, flanked by David and Sandie, as a light rain drizzled down on them, masking the silent tears of the mourners. Afterwards, David invited everyone back to the guesthouse for a light sandwich lunch.

Mabel had been a very proud woman, much like herself, Gloria realised. Perhaps she hadn't needed any help or assistance at the beginning of her downhill spiral. Perhaps Mabel had thought she could cope without bothering her busy-busy family. But it was also a shame that her family had pretty much abandoned her to her own devices. If they'd spared the time to visit Mabel, more often, Gloria was thinking on the drive back to Norwich with Jocelyn, they could've seen what was happening to her and got her to a doctor far sooner. Yet Gloria knew hindsight was a marvellous thing.

At least Mabel's family had realised the error of their ways and reconnected with her to give her a happy albeit short period of respite, even if it had come a little late in the day.

Why were some families' lives so darned complicated that it messed up the thread of decency and honour, which Gloria felt should prevail throughout a family's life together? If you can't find a safe haven within the family unit, where can you find it?

'Thank God we've got friends,' said Gloria, hugging Jocelyn, when they got back to Norwich, much later that day. 'And thanks for this, Joss. I won't forget it.'

Gloria, however, had also had a skinful of her own son. She'd wanted to shake him and hug him at the same time. He'd ruined their family life because of his selfish, controlling ways. Even Val seemed to be under his thumb.

But at least Adam and Jessie had turned out grand and had their own ideas. Gloria had found out that Jessie did not want to go to university as her father wished. She wanted to be a hairdresser and have her own salon, one day, in Norwich. But Clegg wouldn't listen to her, the same way he never listened to anyone. *Idle rantings*, he'd called it.

'You're going to uni and that's that!' he'd apparently shouted at her.

Six days after Gloria moved to Sheringham, she got the call they'd all been waiting for. She had a serious buyer for her house. Actually it was a builder who wanted to knock the place about and turn it into four one-bedroom flats. The very thought made Gloria cringe. With all the work that had been done to the house it looked far better than it had ever done and she'd felt sure a family would buy it or at least someone who could see it would make a terrific family home. Gloria wondered what her grandmother would think about her lifelong home being 'knocked about' by a builder. So she said she'd mull this over with Jocelyn and Tilsbury.

'You're not still in touch with that bloody scoundrel are you, Mother?' said a disgruntled Clegg, when she rang him.

'It's none of your bloody business who I knock around with, you little shit!' she'd said, finally losing her cool with him. 'He's my dearest friend, next to Jocelyn. And at least *I've* got friends . . .'

'Well hurry up and make a decision, is all. We need to move on this.'

'I'll go at the pace I choose, is all you need to know!' she said, slamming the phone down, fuming.

Boy, would she like to slap her son!

Well, both Tilsbury and Jocelyn agreed it was her own decision but that it depended on what she intended to do with her life and how she wanted to use the money. At the end of the day it was only bricks and mortar, so did it really matter who did what to it?

Gloria acquiesced, grudgingly, and told Clegg to go ahead and accept the builder's offer.

Clegg responded by saying he wanted to call a family meeting, afterwards, to agree on what was going to happen with Gloria's accommodation and his children's further education. Gloria told him in no uncertain terms what Jessie's intentions about her further education were.

'Oh, so now you think you can tell me how to run my children's lives! Well Jessie is going to uni whether she likes the idea or not –'

'Right, well in that case you're not havin' any of my money to finance their future. Ruin their lives any way you choose to, Clegg, but don't drag me into your battles!' she shouted, slamming the phone down on him again.

The receiver was hardly placed in its cradle when the phone in Gloria's bedroom rang again and she was about to gear up for another round with her infuriating son, when she heard a different voice.

'Why hello, Mrs Frensham, Ron Byrd here, regarding that other little matter you wanted me to sort out.'

Gloria's demeanour changed and she felt charged with life. 'Oh! Wow! It's done already?'

'An agreement has been drawn up, yes!'

Chapter 34

Gloria had asked Ron Byrd if he wouldn't mind accom-panying her to see the place, the very next day. He'd grumbled about it a bit but Gloria reminded him that since he'd already told her he wasn't that busy and since he was the owner's solicitor and had the keys . . .

So they walked through the light, bright rooms in that new first-floor flat near Sheringham town centre, a huge grin filling Gloria's face. She was delighted, thrilled.

She'd never have taken it if it didn't have the lift and it also came with one parking space, even though she didn't drive. It was only a one-bedroom flat but all the rooms were spacious so it didn't feel claustrophobic at all. Plus there was a tiny balcony where she could sit and have an early morning cup of tea if she wished. She couldn't see the sea but her flat overlooked the communal garden, which was landscaped with well-established shrubs and a little garden seating area with a table if she wanted to sit outside with a book and a cuppa at any time.

It was so exciting!

Clegg was sure to go mad but she couldn't let that stop

her. He was always going mad these days. He would probably always go mad in the future. That seemed to be his way, now. But that couldn't be helped. She realised he probably wanted to put her somewhere far away, so it didn't interfere with their lives. And that could not happen either. Although she was very touched that both Adam and Jessie had said they'd visit her wherever she ended up.

'Must say, Grandma, we think Dad has treated you horribly and we can't understand why. He's just stupid sometimes. But Adam and I'll still come and see ya. We missed you, growing up. Mum's sister, Auntie Ida, used to babysit us, which was okay but she never let us stay up late or anything.'

'Ha, ha. But mebbe I wouldn't've either, darlin'!'

'Oh, we think we'd've got away with things with you.' Jessie grinned sweetly. 'But not with Aunt Ida!'

Anyway, the flat was perfect for her. And she knew her grandchildren would love visiting her there, too.

So she said yes to Ron Byrd and then he said he'd get the lease all finalised with his client.

Chapter 35

With the sale of her house imminent, she'd taken the little flat, two streets back from the seafront at Sheringham, to rent for six months. Jocelyn had kindly helped her contact everyone and put her in touch with a home store to get new furniture sorted out. This would then take her until early spring to decide what she wanted to do after that. It was the best idea she and Jocelyn could think of, in order to give her more breathing space, whilst a lot of things were going on around her.

The next thing on her agenda, Gloria decided, was to arrange her eightieth birthday party.

Neither Val nor Clegg had mentioned it and she thought her son had either forgotten about it or was spittin' the dummy about things. Either way she was not fussed. She wasn't tiptoeing around her boy any longer. Enough was enough. Plus with the sale of her house and her own money in her pocket for once, it would mean that she could darned well do exactly as she pleased. She didn't need Clegg's permission to enjoy her own life.

And it pleased her to be able to arrange her own birthday

with the help of the Sheringham hotel. She had no intention, either, of inviting Clegg and Val. Not unless the situation with them changed sometime soon and she couldn't see that happening in this lifetime. But she was a mum, so she'd leave it open for them to work it all out and do the right thing before it was too late.

Adam and Jessie said they wanted to help her, so Adam – a whizz with computers – helped her design the party invitations and Jessie used Gloria's new bank card to have them printed and paid to send them all off. They were sworn to secrecy so that they wouldn't tell their parents.

'Adult problems are tricky little devils,' Gloria had said by way of explanation.

But when the little RSVP notes included with the invitations started coming back, Gloria couldn't believe it. All the Eastbourne lot had replied to her invites. They'd ALL replied. They couldn't all make it, of course, but how kind to actually take the trouble to send the replies back.

Out of everyone from that trip to Eastbourne, and all the exchanged telephone numbers and addresses, Joe was coming, along with Vittori, Dot, Florence, Freda and four of the others! And, of course, Jocelyn, Marvin and Tilsbury said they wouldn't miss it for the world.

'Wouldn't mind meetin' them new friends of yours, Glor,' Jocelyn wrote on the reply. 'Me and Marv used to think about doin' one of them coach trips. But we never got round to it.'

The hotel on the seafront in Sheringham was chosen as

the venue and they informed Gloria they would be doing a special rate for the party-goers so that everyone could stay the night of the party, if they wished to.

'Well, love, you've been such a good customer of ours, this year, that we knew we had to do right by you,' explained Charlie, the manager. 'So you'll be gettin' a reduced rate for the rooms as well as the meal. Plus I think we can get some free bottles of bubbly for the toast too. Now, did you say you'd be payin' for the lot yourself or will it be individual bills?'

'Oh thanks, ducks! That's champion! And, yes, you heard right. I'm treatin' EVERYONE to EVERYTHING. And that's ALL my friends, both old and new. They're all pensioners themselves and don't get given much for free. So I want them to come along and enjoy themselves without worryin' about stuff like bills for a change.'

Of course, Gloria did realise that if for any reason the sale of her house didn't go through as planned, she wouldn't be able to pay for anyone to enjoy her party. But that didn't worry her unduly, because if she couldn't pay, Clegg would certainly have to, *as he'd forgotten to take the credit card off her.*

Chapter 36

The Sheringham hotel had decked out their back room a real treat for Gloria with eightieth birthday bunting lining the walls and helium balloons in pink trying to make a break for the ceiling.

The finger buffet was piled high, ranging from curried chicken vol au vents and potato wedges with dips to mixed meats off the bone and prawn skewers. The birthday cake in the centre had been especially baked on the premises by the chef. It was shaped into an 80 with white icing and chocolate buttons dotted about, on top, as a fun request from Gloria. She'd wanted Smarties for the colour aspect but was then reminded of people's dentures!

On the afternoon of the party, Gloria proudly introduced her old friends to her new. It was a feeling she liked, being in charge for once. Plus all the guests she'd invited were lovely, lovely people, so she knew it was going to be a fantastic occasion.

She wore a new dress she'd bought especially, with tiny turquoise flowers set against a white background and three-quarter-length sleeves that she thought looked pretty and fresh. Carefully clipped to the front of her dress was an eight-ieth birthday badge that said, Young at Heart 80, off her birthday card from Adam and Jessie.

'Here look, Joe. I've got yer locket on. It was a grand surprise, I can tell you. Prettiest thing I ever been given, it is, ducks. Thanks a million. And these are my best mates, Jocelyn, Tilsbury and his bro' Marvin. Told you the story, there, haven't I?' She chuckled, leaving the four of them with her eyebrows raised.

She went up to a man standing nervously by himself.

'Thanks for coming, Ron. You've helped me out no end so I want you to enjoy yourself this afternoon. There's plenty of food and drink too. Look, let me introduce ya to someone you probably haven't seen in a while. She's here with her ex-husband and her new boyfriend and – get this – they happen to be brothers! Yeah. It's certainly very interestin' round these parts! Ha, ha!'

'Why, Ron Byrd! Well I never thought I'd be rubbin' shoul-ders with you at any party!' said Jocelyn with a big smile. 'You've been helpin' our Glor, though, haven't ya?'

Sixties' music blared out from the disco speakers the hotel had hired and the revellers were foot tapping or making brave attempts at modern moves on the dance floor, encouraged by Jessie.

A smiling Gloria went up to Tilsbury and hugged him. His face was clean-shaven and she even smelled a hint of after-shave. She was pleased he'd scrubbed up for the occasion.

'So, ducks, bit of a change of events from a few months back! And um thanks for them little gold star earrings you gave me. Jocelyn said you've been savin' up for them for ages. Probably the only things you ain't nicked in a while, too, huh?'

Tilsbury hid his blush with a huge grin. 'Pleased ya appreciate them. Thought you'd like 'em.'

'I do, ducks!'

'Must say you're looking good for eighty, old gal!'

'Oi, less of the old, Tils. Think I've found my mojo or summat. Feel more alive than I have for years. It started with that chilly swim that day. And everythin' else that happened, happened because of that crazy swim. That's why we're here now. That's why I've got me little flat, here. Because of you.'

She kissed his cheek.

'So you're not bowled over by that Joe then. Seems keen on ya.'

'No, Tils. He's not keen on me. He misses his Carol. They were wed for sixty-one years. Think it did him good to get me that locket. He wasn't thinking about his Carol for once. I were thrilled with it too, mind. Ain't never had nothing that beautiful before. Givin' things is good for the soul, Tils. But everythin' that's happened to me of late is down to you. You started that ball rollin', ya did, I'm happy to say.'

'That's right. Blame me for everything!' Tilsbury grinned.

Gloria took his hand. 'But it's a good blame, isn't it? Anyway, I want a word with ya. Did you sort summat out with social

207

services about yer accommodation? Jocelyn told me you'd been having problems with them.'

Tilsbury shrugged. 'I'm not an unwed youngster with six kids in tow nor an old boy with dementia yet, is all. They've put me on a waiting list but told me it could be a long time before anything comes up. But it's a start. Things had to change. I've been bumming around for far too long, Glor. Should've got summat sorted years ago, like our Lily,' he said referring to his sister. 'But life happens, as you know.'

At that moment there was a loud clanging and everyone turned to see Charlie, the manager, banging a gong and saying it was time to propose a toast.

'Grab yer glasses, lads and lasses. It's time to toast the good health of this young lady here who is eighty today! Happy birthday to Gloria!'

'Happy birthday, Gloria!' they all said obediently.

'She wants me to propose a toast to all her friends and new-found friends as well. And tells me the next time she sees you all will be back down in Eastbourne on yer holidays next July! So cheers to that, everyone!'

Shouts and whoops went up. Everyone clapped. Someone popped a balloon. Freda patted Gloria on her back.

'Wow, love. You're coming back again then?'

'Course I am, ducks. Wouldn't miss a treat like that for nothin'. I loved it. Plus I've not been on one of those fast RIB tours yet down the seafront!'

'Ha, ha. So pleased, Gloria,' said Joe. 'It would be a real

shame if this was the last time we got to see ya.'

Joe walked over to Charlie and had a quick word.

'Okay, lads and lasses, just one more toast, from Joe and the rest of the Eastbourne Holiday Team and that's to say a big thank you for inviting them all to your party and for the marvellous spread you put on for them and many thanks, also, for paying for their rooms so everyone could stay the night. So cheers and thanks again.'

'Cheers and thanks, Gloria! You're a good 'un,' everyone yelled.

They all raised their glasses and cheered, and it was at that precise moment Clegg and Val walked through the door.

Chapter 37

Adam looked sheepish.

'I'm sorry, Gran. Mum still cleans my room, you see. Oh, don't look at me like that, Grandma – I do it myself, sometimes! But she saw one of the invites.'

Gloria's frown relaxed. She didn't feel angry with Adam. It wasn't his fault. Perhaps it was wrong to have included the children in her scheme. Their loyalty was with their mum and dad, as it should be, of course. And, well, at least Clegg and Val had bothered to show up. Possibly Clegg decided to come because Gloria was doing something that wasn't costing them anything for once. But Gloria understood that.

'There's food and drinks over there, Val. Help yourself, love.'

Val reached forward and gave Gloria a cursory hug. 'He *had* forgotten, you know. But he insisted we were coming,' Val whispered.

'S'all right, love. Don't really mind now you're both here. The kids'll like it. It's family stuff anyway, innit, love?'

Clegg stood in front of Gloria but she put a sharp finger up.

'Don't say a ruddy thing, son. This is my party and I'll not have any argy-bargy. Now go and get summat to eat and we'll talk later.'

She walked over to Dot, who was wearing a pale blue polka dot dress two sizes too big for her. Perhaps she liked wearing dresses with a bit of room in them.

'So how're you liking Sheringham then, ducks?'

'I'm likin' it fine. We all went for a walk round when our families dropped us off this morning. Pretty little place but the sea is *not* the same nice colour as Eastbourne. Here, but your mates Jocelyn and Marvin say they're thinking of coming on the next trip?'

'Yes they told me they fancied it. They'd love it, too. Oh, 'scuse me, Dot. I just want a quick word with my friend Tils. See ya in five.'

Gloria caught hold of Tilsbury's arm and whisked him outside.

'Here, you ambushing me?'

'I am, Tils, and the reason for it is simple. I would like you to move into my new flat with me. It's only one bedroom but it's a large room and it'll take twin beds and –'

'Hang on! Slow down, love. What're ya sayin'?'

'Look, Tils. Now my house is sold and I've got me money sorted out, I'm renting that flat for six months to see if I like it round here. Well, I know I do, already. I love it lots. Anyways there's no reason for you to still be dossin' when you can stay here with me. But only if ya want. I don't want to be pushin' ya into summat ya don't want to do. But I think it's a great solution. Plus you're me best friend, apart from Jocelyn, and we could have some crackin' times here.'

'Yup. But that's only potentially for six months. What happens after that? Me whole life has been stopping off places for a while and then movin' on. I'm getting a bit old for all that now, love.'

'Yes but I've got the option to buy it outright, after that. And it's not one of them buy-to-rent schemes for the elderly. It's a proper normal purchase, so it'd be totally mine. So that means no more renting and it'll be mine forever. Just like before. Only better. And I really fancy doin' just that. I think I'm gonna love livin' here all the time, Tils. And I think you would too if you just thought about it. Look, I don't want ya to give me an answer today. Just think about it. Think about what you want outta life too, Tils. I know you're a bit of a wanderin' soul, ducks. And you could still wander a bit, if ya want. But it'd be somewhere to rest yer head, at the end of the day.'

Tilsbury nodded slowly. 'Aye, I'll have a think about it, love. I've been thinking about a lot of things these last few months. I'll let ya know but thanks for that, love.'

* * *

'So what do ya think, Val? Pretty nice, innit?'

Val admitted that Gloria's new home was very nice indeed.

213

'Yes, you've done very well here, Gloria. It's bright. It's modern. Easy to keep looking fresh and clean, isn't it, Clegg, love?'

Clegg hadn't said much since he'd arrived in Sheringham. He wasn't openly impressed by much under ordinary circumstances. Gloria thought it was because he wasn't into lots of change and suddenly everything around him was changing. And not necessarily for the better, in his eyes.

Yet that's how life went sometimes, Gloria knew. But she was interested to learn what he had to say.

'All I'll say to you, Mother, is this. If it all starts again – if you start draggin' a whole load more crap in because you want to give it a home for some crazy notion or other – I will be exertin' my right to put you away somewhere safe. It's all nice and pretty, this, I'll give you that. But we don't have the time nor inclination to deal with any more crap from you. It cost me a bomb last time. And I'm not puttin' up with any more of your nonsense ever again.'

Gloria nodded thoughtfully.

'It's a shame nothing loving ever comes outta yer mouth, Cleggy. I mean I'd like to think I've changed. I know I heard what they said at Green's Nursin' Home. I don't feel as though I want to start draggin' crap in again. I hope I don't. But where is yer compassion for my situation, son? It's a wonder Adam and Jessie grew up to be the lovely people they have, with you spillin' yer guts at every turn –'

'Yes. About them, Mother?'

'What about them, Clegg?'

214

'Their future. Their education? You can't cut them out just because you and I don't get on!'

'My God! What is wrong with you, boy? Is life all about money to you? Not about people and feelings? Well if that's the case, all I've got say to you, Cleggy, is this: when they come to me individually and discuss what they want to do with their lives – and I make a point about the word *THEIR* – I will make a decision about what *I'm* going to do for them. You'll get no say in it. And just to let you know, I've already had an initial conversation with both of them. So they both know the situation.'

Val nodded. 'I agree with that, Cleggy, I'm afraid. Jessie really wants to be a hairdresser. So I'm with both of them on that score. So that's great, Gloria. Thank you for that.'

'You're welcome, Val. I think you and I should keep some lines of conversation open in the future, but here's the thing: as for you, Cleggy, I don't want to see you or hear from you regarding anything over the next few months. And yes that includes Christmas,' Gloria said, pausing to take a deep breath. 'You've never invited me round to yours for a Christmas meal since Arthur went. What a shame, keeping me from the kids. What a shame keeping me out of your lives. It's affected how I feel about things now. But I will let you know this one thing: I had a look at some of yer paperwork when I got back from me travels. So I know how much ya got outstandin' on yer mortgage. It's not so much. So my Christmas present to the both of youse, because I'm still yer ruddy mother at the end of the day, is that I'll pay it off. But then you'll see no more of my money. That's it. And I do think that you, Val, should stick up for yourself more with Cleggy and not let him take advantage. He needs to learn some manners. He's always been a bit of a twat. Now get out of my house!'

Chapter 38

When the sun shone down on the east coast the sea could become a deep teal colour. It would probably never be that Mediterranean turquoise or Eastbourne blue but it certainly looked welcoming enough.

It was where Gloria lived now. And Sheringham had easily become her home, as she'd known all along that it would. She loved it here. She often walked down the front with Jessie or Adam and had even been pleased to take that same walk with Val on a few occasions. They got on so much better now.

Unfortunately, Gloria hadn't seen Tilsbury in a while and he hadn't said whether he intended to move in with her or not. But, she realised, she might just need to give him more time to work that one out for himself. Maybe the idea of putting down roots would be a big thing for Tilsbury to have to deal with because he'd never done it before.

However, Gloria enjoyed her walks with Val now. They sometimes went for a cuppa and even managed to go shopping together on one occasion, which Gloria had thoroughly enjoyed. She'd secretly wished she'd had a daughter after Cleggy. Partly to even the odds, but more so she could've shared things like cosy shopping trips with her. Val had started opening up to her, about things, now they were friendly with each other. She'd also agreed that Clegg was a bully but admitted their rows never changed how he viewed the world or life. He would always be his own inimitable self whether the rest of them liked that fact or not.

'Paying off our mortgage has taken away some of our headaches. We've paid off a few other debts that were mounting as well. So I'm full of gratitude for that, Gloria. Thank you!'

'Well sure, Val. We've none of us ever been rich or had money, love. But when my grandmother left me that house I never imagined all the grief it would cause nor how much it'd sell for. It's more money than I could ever hope for. And I didn't want to just cling on to it for myself, you know. I wanted to share it. Give a bit to others. Of course I wanted to help me family and you're all me family even though there have been problems. We're not unique in havin' problems, though, are we? All families go through it. But I can't get me head round how mean Cleggy is to me. I've even proved I'm not dragging stuff straight back into me flat, so why does he still resent me? Why is there never a kind word from him? And it does hurt, even though I don't show it, love. Have you any inklin' as to why he's like it, love?'

Val pulled a face and looked down at her feet as she walked.

'The one thing I do know about him is that he's never really got on with authority, of any description. That stint in the army might have made him bullish but he was lucky enough to get a decent job, afterwards, as security guard at his company. But perhaps it's too rigid for him. Perhaps he should've got a different type of job when he left. But that's all he could get at the time. Problem is, there's no creativity or friendliness there per se and they certainly don't go out to buy cakes when it's someone's birthday! I personally think he no longer wants to be the big guy that everybody goes to for help. When we were first married it was all so different. He was more light-hearted and joyful then. Yet he's not too bad with the kids.'

'You're right, love. Life was better for all of us, in those days, when Arthur was alive. It fell off after that, though, didn't it?'

'It did. And I don't know how it happened, I'm sorry to say, Gloria. Maybe it was the death of his father that did it. Though I never saw him upset about losin' his dad. But men are like that, sometimes, aren't they? Keep things to themselves. And even though, for me, nursing is totally consuming, I probably should've paid more attention to what was happening to us all. But until your electrics blew, I didn't even realise there was a real problem. And as for us not inviting you round for Christmas, I guess I'm just as much to blame, you see. But we were always so busy. Too busy to see what was going on right under our noses, I guess.' Val sighed, apologetically.

Gloria nodded in agreement. 'Yes, well, I'm afraid I did think you were partly to blame for that, ducks. I did feel you should've insisted on havin' me round.'

219

'I know, Gloria. It was wrong of me. But unfortunately Clegg's exact words were, "She don't wash no more. Stinks to high heaven!" And I did think it would've made everyone feel extremely uncomfortable, I'm sorry to say. Clegg's a proud man – stupid sometimes, granted – but extremely proud and I don't think your predicament sat well with him. In short, if I'm honest, I don't think he knew how to deal with it.'

'Uh-huh. Well I'm sorry I made you all embarrassed, love.'

'Well I'm sorry about things too, Gloria. But everything's been sorted out now and you *will* be coming for Christmas with us this year – if you'd like. I *will* be puttin' my foot down about that in future!'

'Well thank you, Val, but I think we'll play future Christmases by ear. I'm going to help out at a soup kitchen, this year. Thought I'd like to give summat back to folk in a way that's useful.'

Val stopped and stared at Gloria, as if seeing her in a new light.

'Oh wow! What a marvellous thing to do, Gloria! Jessie and I did that one year – she wanted to do it. And they all get to join up and have a meal together, afterwards, don't they?'

'They've said so, so I'm lookin' forward to that. Plus they say they'll come get me and drop me back later. So I'm pleased about that, too.'

'Well that's inspirin' stuff, Gloria. You should feel proud of yourself for doin' that.'

'Aye, lass. I am, actually.'

Chapter 39

'So you've not heard from him either then, ducks?' Gloria said, when she rang Jocelyn.

'No I ain't, Glor, and it's not like him, is it!' said Jocelyn worriedly. 'I mean we even miss him nickin' stuff! I'm even thinkin' about ringin' the police, just in case summat's happened to him.'

'Gawd. It's worryin'. So how long's he been gone, Joss?'

'Near after you moved in, proper. Couple of months. It's a while back, now. Did youse have a row or summat?'

Gloria tutted. 'Nah. We've never been the rowin' sort. I might raise me voice sometimes but I never row, ducks. But, you see, I did ask him to move in with me, again. Like before, if he wanted, for a roof over his head. He never gave me an answer though.'

'Yes he did tell us,' Jocelyn admitted. 'And – despite our differences, Glor – I did think it was a good idea. Think he expected *me* to invite him to stay but it's difficult with Marvin and me now. Not that I wouldn't invite him but it's just a bit awkward.'

'Yeh it is, Joss. He says it doesn't suit him dossin' about all the time now. But I've no idea what he intends to do now the social won't help him.'

'I'm not sure either, love. Anyways, I've got to be off. Goin' to the pictures tonight with Marvin. Ain't done that in years, love. But pleased you're gettin' on with Val a bit more now. It'll ease things between ya. Ta-ra, love.'

Gloria put the phone down.

She was worried about Tilsbury. If she sat and thought about it, she didn't really know him now. Perhaps she never had. She didn't know what he got up to when they weren't together and Jocelyn admitted she was equally in the dark about that. He'd never been one for hobbies when they'd been younger. He'd lived and worked and gone out around Norwich all his life, apart from that stint after they split up when they'd been sweethearts. But he'd never been one for wanting to travel much or explore, after he came back from India with his dad and siblings. He was a loner and quite happy to be independent and self-sufficient, and if that included living rough, so be it.

Gloria made a decision.

She knew Jocelyn said she was thinking of calling the police but she was on her way out, now, with Marvin. Sadly everyone was getting on with their lives without much concern for Tilsbury. He'd always been flitting around, in the background, somewhere. But now, even though he'd not been seen for about eight weeks, no one seemed especially concerned.

Yet that man had set her on the road to self-discovery this year. Her life had completely changed because of one selfless act from him – a simple trip out for afternoon tea.

So Gloria knew she had to help him somehow. Okay, but where to begin?

She started by ringing the police. They said no one had been found or was in their cells by his name. Did she have a recent photo? *Nobody* had a photo of Tilsbury. She wasn't even sure there was one in existence!

Then she tried the local hospitals. What if he'd been run over by a car or been in a fight that wasn't of his doing? Or what if – saints preserve us – he'd just dropped down dead, somewhere? Again, the hospital staff confirmed there was no one in their care of that name.

Next she tried Shelter and even though they knew of him they said they hadn't seen him in a while. So she tried social services and was put through to a good many departments before someone mentioned that an elderly chap, of that name, had been to see them, recently, about being housed.

'Yes and you didn't want to house him did you?' Gloria suddenly snapped, surprising herself.

'Look, it's not that we don't want to house people but he does have an address, doesn't he?'

'Well, yes and no! That's his ex-wife's address. But he hasn't lived there in twenty-some-odd years, ducks! He just uses that address for letters and his pension. He's been dossin' around for all the time since he's left her, in parks and under bridges and the like! It ain't right. And you lot can't be arsed wantin' to help him.'

'No, you've got it wrong. We do help people in need. It's just that we haven't got homes for everyone and we do have to prioritise. But we've put him on a list and –'

'Yes but he'll be dead by the time that list comes round! He's over eighty, ducks!'

Gloria slammed the phone down, annoyed. But she'd discovered the last time he'd been in there was when they put him on that list; just before her party, two months ago.

So that was that then. Who else was there she could ring? There were no other services she could call and he didn't really have any other close friends that she or Jocelyn were aware of.

Think, Gloria!

Aha!

Why yes, of course! There *was* one other person who'd probably know . . .

Chapter 40

Lying on her chaise longue in the cool conservatory, fronds of ferns and ivy hanging down, Lily did not rush to pick up the phone. Everything hurt these days, so it didn't help matters to rush.

'Why, Gloria! How lovely to hear from you!' said Lily, as her hand finally snicked the receiver from its cradle, on its last ring.

Gloria hadn't spoken to Tilsbury's famous sister in years but she was so concerned about him, she came straight to the point.

'Well, hello, love. Look I'd love to talk to ya but I'm worried about Tilsbury. No one's heard from him or seen him since my party. I don't suppose you've seen him recently have you, ducks?'

'Ha, ha! But you know what my brother's like, Gloria. Not a man of many words, opting in and out of life when he chooses, I'll give you that. But he has brought me up to date with all your exploits and he did tell me you'd offered him a roof over his head at your new place. I said he should accept. After all, he's not got a home to speak of has he?'

'No he ain't, ducks. He does have his name on a list with the social though. So at least he's done summat about things.'

'Yes I'm pleased he finally decided to do something about that. It's long overdue, of course, him bouncin' around from pillar to post all his ruddy life. Well, okay, to put your mind at rest, I can let you know he's out and about, Gloria. He told me he needed some space to sort his life out. Anybody'd think he was a youngster taking a gap year out, the way he was talking, instead of a silly old fogey! But, well, I think he was a little disillusioned with the outcome at the social. So, anyway, he came and stayed with me for a week and then off he went to Scotland.'

'*Scotland?* But he reckons he doesn't like travellin'.'

Lily laughed, shrilly.

'Not any more, he doesn't. Granted! But he said it was one place he'd always wanted to go to but never got round to visiting. I think he's got an old mate up there, he hasn't seen for years. But he says you inspired him with all your adventures and so he said before he drops down dead in some obscure place, he wanted to follow that one dream. He asked me if I'd pay for it and I told him it would be my lifelong Christmas gift to him. We've never been ones for exchanging gifts of any kind. But um I've got breast cancer, you see, and er not really long to go now, so I told him to go enjoy himself, life being short.'

'Oh, dear Lord, Lily, I'm so sorry to hear that, love.'

'Oh don't worry, Gloria. We all have our crosses to bear.

But I've had a fabulous life. Father was clever enough to make a good living from the railroads in India, as you know. So when he returned to Blighty he was a very wealthy man. I know I didn't do so much to speak of, apart from those six years as arts director for that fashion house in London –'

'Oh but you were fabulous, Lily! And in all the local and national papers. You won awards. We all thought you were great.'

'Ha, ha. Well, thank you! Yes, Gloria, I did have some fun, didn't I? And my "giving back" thing, of course, was that voluntary stint I did for a year in Kenya, helping out with that government programme where they constructed new schools, after I met my Brian. You'd have laughed seein' me on roofs holding the joists, while Brian hammered the nails in. *Imagine!* And toileting in holes in the ground. My goodness! Not like me at all, is it, that, Gloria! Ah well. But I didn't want people to think I was just born into a life of luxury. We weren't well-off when Mum died, until Father did his India stint anyway, were we? Oh, just a minute Gloria.' Lily broke off to have a few sips of water.

Gloria knew Lily had been housebound for a while but hadn't known the reason for that and Tilsbury hadn't told her either. She supposed that Lily had few people to chat to or confide in these days – just like Tilsbury – but Gloria was happy that Lily felt the need to offload to her. They'd not talked in a long time. And anyway, Gloria knew that Tilsbury was safe and okay now.

227

'Go on, Lily,' she encouraged.

'Yes, of course Gloria. Oh – er, what was I saying? Oh yes, I was going to say that Tilsbury, Marvin and I had a great time in India with our father. School there was a bit crap until we were home-schooled. But he took us everywhere. He showed us the good and the ugly of that country, as well as places like Delhi and the Taj Mahal. It was an amazing experience and, of course, it influenced some of what I did in London, as you know. However, it unsettled Tilsbury when we got back. He was the talk of his clique for a while. But when they all went off to college or got jobs he thought it was okay to just bum around, doing a bit of bar work and the like.'

'Aye, it caused some trouble, it did,' Gloria admitted, thinking about that time.

'It's a shame though, Gloria, 'cos even though Tilsbury took after Father with a good brain in his head, he basically pissed his inheritance up the wall, as they say. Now, if memory serves me, he got a job as time-served carpenter for about six years when he was with Jocelyn, didn't he? He had terrific prospects with the company he worked for. But when they split up he lost it big time. And it cost him his job too, didn't it, clowning about and fallin' off that ladder, as you know. And then, of course, his back was bad for a while. But what did he do afterwards? Well, he didn't go get another job did he! Nope. It was back to bumming around, again, which lost him some cracking opportunities.'

Lily paused with a sigh. 'You know, I do love him, Gloria, but he could've made so much more out of his life. At least our Marvin had regular work driving taxis, back in the day. Anyway, enough of my senile rambling. It just gets to me sometimes, that's all. And that's why I think he should take you up on your very kind offer, Gloria. Well, I'm eighty-four and have outlived most of my friends and done everything I wanted to do in life. Can't ask for much more than that, can you?'

'No you can't, love. Well, it was nice to catch up with you, after all this time. And be sure to tell Tilsbury we're all missing him, when you see him next. I'm pleased he's all right and enjoyin' himself and best regards to you too, Lily. If you ever want to talk about owt just pick up the phone, love. I'm in every night.'

'Why thank you, Gloria. I might just do that one night. Love and kisses. Bye, bye!'

Chapter 41

The central heating in her new flat, now it was December, was a joy. There was always hot water on tap, as well as the fact she had a bath with a shower over the top, so she actually had a *choice* as to how she could bathe! Hee, hee, *such* luxury! *And* she could afford to eat whatever she wanted, although she'd never been one for expensive tastes. She had her weekly shop delivered now, too. Val had helped her set that up with one of the stores. So she really had nothing else to worry about.

But the fact that Tilsbury had chosen not to visit or ring Gloria since her eightieth birthday party niggled her. And even though she now knew where he was she would have to wait until he contacted her. They'd always chatted about all and sundry in the past. It seemed strange to think he didn't want to discuss whatever was going on with him now. Oh well. Gloria knew she'd just have to be patient, even though she did wonder if things were *really* okay with him.

Aside from missing Tilsbury, she secretly thought she'd have given up *everything* just for one of those half-hour visits she used to get from her bolshie son, when she lived in her old house with all her hoardings. Gloria felt she'd come a long way since that time. And yet Clegg hadn't seemed to want to reconnect with her, at all, despite all the changes she'd made and despite evidence of her new clutter-free flat. She was still his mum, after all. Didn't that *mean* something to him?

Of course, she never said anything to Val or the kids. She had wondered, though, if Clegg, in a moment of revulsion at the way he'd treated her, would suddenly ring her, all apologetic. She also wondered how quickly she'd take him back into her arms, if that was the case. It saddened her to think that they hadn't hugged or exchanged any form of affection in *years*.

Val had told Gloria his moods seemed to be getting worse and he was even snapping at all of them, at home, as well now. So Gloria didn't truly believe he was going to change for the better, any time soon. Ah well, she could but live in hope.

Anyway Christmas was a mere six days away and she'd soon be doing her stint at the Soup Kitchen in Norwich. She'd been down to meet the other helpers, the week previously, care of Val.

'Now I just want to be sure you're totally certain you want to do this, Gloria. There's all sorts of people go there; some very nice, I might add, but some who just want to cause trouble. Might be a bit much for you is all I'm sayin'.'

'I appreciate your concern, Val, love. But I'm goin' to give it a go. I want to do summat different this year. Don't want to gorge on food when there's them around me that can't. You see, Tilsbury's had need of their services from time to time and said how many sad cases there were over there. So I'd like to do my bit.'

'Well, as long as you know what you're doing. Clegg says it's disgusting, people expecting hand-outs. But we all know how narrow-minded he is!' she'd said with a sad smile.

'Well, thanks for bringing me over, anyway, love,' said Gloria. 'I shouldn't be too long, if you can wait. It's very kind of you.'

She was surprised at how friendly and comfortable the shelter was that she was asked to visit. It was their head office but it was also somewhere people could call into, to get a few hours off the streets or to talk to someone in a friendly environment, as well as get a bed for the night, if they were in dire need.

'Trouble is, no one knows what dish life is about to deal,' said Mark, currently in charge of the volunteers. 'You never know just how much crap you can bear until life serves it to you. And the people we see and house or feed, here, are from all walks of life. There are people with kids trying to juggle life below the living wage, or they're physically challenged or suffer from mental illness or are otherwise very vulnerable. There are even people who once had everything and suddenly lost their job and everything else with it. We can offer advice or blankets to people if they intend to continue living rough. Or we can offer a shower or room for the night or longer if they wish to commit to trying to sort their lives out.'

'Yeah, I know. It's a callin' offering that sort of help, ducks. I know that. I've got a mate who's been to you a few times and that's why I want to help over the Christmas period. I know I'm a bit past it, love. But I still want to help. I've got some good thermals and the like now. I haven't always had a good life, myself, you see and it's only recently I've been helped by some lovely people. So I know I want to do this,' Gloria explained. 'Must say, though, it's lovely and homely here, too.'

Mark grinned back. 'That's very kind, Gloria. Yes, we like to be thought of as approachable. A lot of those we help have had rough beginnings so every bit of friendship and warmth helps them to open up and feel that they're cared for and not wasting anyone's time.'

'Right. So, if you're happy, I'll see you for the three days 24th, 25th and 26th then.'

Mark shook Gloria's hand.

'Only if it's not too much for you and if it is let me know. Here's my card. But do not feel you have to do the whole three days. Any help you can give us will be very appreciated by all the other helpers and the homeless people themselves, as you'll see on the day. And we also wear one of these yellow bands, diagonally, across our chests so the clients can see who we are. So this one is for you.'

Gloria proudly took the yellow band.

Val and Adam and Jessie all turned up to drop Gloria off on the 24th of December outside the premises for the homeless. But to Gloria's surprise, Val went to park the car and then returned with her children to help Gloria on her first night at the Soup Kitchen.

'You didn't have to do this!' Gloria said to Val.

'Actually Adam and Jessie said they *wanted* to help you on your first night and I thought: What the hell. So I'm here too!'

Gloria was touched and proud of her family wanting to share this experience with her. She wiped a tear away, with her sleeve. What a shame, though, that Clegg couldn't commit to being a better, more loving family member.

Chapter 42

The first night had been splendid, flanked by her grand-children and Val, helping her and the other volunteers serve soup to the homeless. Jessie and Adam had brought along sparkly garlands for the other volunteers to wear around their necks, like a scarf. And Val had baked a stack of mince pies to give to everybody, volunteers as well as the homeless people. They'd softly sung Christmas carols, encouraging everyone to join in, and had a natter and a laugh and joke with everyone they came into contact with.

Val recognised a man who often turned up at A&E after a fight or three. And Gloria even met another old lady who'd had problems with hoarding, in her past, but was now getting help from an organisation recently set up by a local hospital that recognised the detrimental effects similar age-related problems had on society's elderly.

'I used to be quite agoraphobic. But I'm here with that woman over there. The one there, in the blue coat. It's taken a while and I'm okay if I come out, with her, at night. The world doesn't seem so big and scary at night. But she started the ball rolling for me when my daughter got her to come round and have a chat with me. I'd refused all help before that, you see. Silly of me, I see that now. But at the time I didn't see what I was doing. Anyway, she's helping me to start sorting things out at the moment. It's slow going. I think we'll get there. Least she helped me understand why I was doing it. I used to be so lonely.'

'Aye, loneliness is a terrible thing,' Gloria agreed. 'We build walls around ourselves. But trouble is we're locking ourselves in, not keeping folk out. Anyway, very nice to have met you, love. Have you got one of those mince pies yet? Give her a mince pie, Val.'

Gloria and her family's upbeat demeanour had rubbed off on everybody and they'd been made to feel very welcome both by the other volunteers and the homeless people as well.

Mark the manager had been right: it really was quite inspiring for Gloria to be able to give some of her time to those who'd needed it most. She told Val she thought both Adam and Jessie would've benefited from having done something so selfless over the Christmas period.

But by the end of the second night, Christmas Day, Gloria was beginning to feel drained.

She'd had a lazy morning, around her new sparkling Christmas tree, which she'd decorated with tiny glass angels Val had helped her choose. Then she'd sat in her cosy dressing gown, with a cup of tea, opening all the cards from her friends – both new and old – as well as gifts from her grandchildren and Val. Val had written *With Love from Val & Clegg* on hers.

Adam and Jessie had got her a big box of chocolates and Val got her some toiletries. These might seem like ordinary gifts to some people but Gloria hadn't had more than a small Christmas card in the past from Clegg, so these gifts felt heart-warming to her.

Brr. But it was going to be another cold night, going off to serve soup to the homeless. However, she had no intention of letting Mark and the other volunteers down, even though it was so lovely and warm in her own flat. So she dutifully donned her coat and hat and gloves and awaited the arrival of Mark in his Mini.

The volunteers rubbed their mittened hands and stamped their feet to keep warm on that second night. It wasn't quite as cheery as when her grandchildren and Val had helped out. But the volunteers still wore their glitzy sparkly 'scarves' and there were still some mince pies left over from the night before.

Between them they'd served ninety-six soups on the first night and Gloria'd just served the one hundred and sixty-eighth person on Christmas Day when she noticed potential trouble from one of the men further up the line. There tended to be more men than women in the lines, she'd noticed, seeking hot food.

He was brusque, unshaven and carried an empty vodka bottle that he was brandishing about while swearing at everyone around him. Mark had temporarily popped inside the shelter to get more soup, which left three women, including Gloria, by themselves, serving.

'So what soooup we got tonight then, missus?' he slurred to Gloria, swerving towards her.

'We can do chicken or broccoli and Stilton, love,' she replied, cautiously, remaining calm, as she'd been instructed to do on her induction night.

'Oh sod off! We had that last week! It's Christmas Day for God's sake – ain't you got summat better than that for our Christmas dinner? We had curried parsnip last year!'

Just then a very different voice answered him, stepping in next to Gloria and taking the ladle from her hands.

'No, we ain't, mate. So it's bloody chicken or bloody broccoli and Stilton! *MATE!*'

Gloria turned, surprised, at the sound of his voice. Then her eyes filled with tears as she looked at the man standing next to her. He looked different somehow – leaner, more confident. She also detected a faint trace of the aftershave he'd used at her eightieth birthday bash.

'Of course, the other option is take it or bloody leave it, mate!' added her saviour.

'Oh all right then, mate. Keep yer 'air on, I was just sayin'. I'll 'ave chicken then.'

'I think that's the most swearin' you've ever done, in all the time I've known you,' Gloria whispered softly, smiling.

When Mark reappeared Tilsbury told him what had just happened and said he was taking Gloria home, although she did protest at that.

But Mark smiled encouragingly.

'No. You've done us proud, Gloria. You and your family were great last night and you've done more than your fair share tonight. So please, go home and enjoy the rest of your Christmas.'

The other volunteers and most of the people in the line cheered and clapped and thanked her for her time helping them all.

'Thanks, Gloria!'

'Happy Christmas, love!'

'Thanks for everythin', love. Merry Christmas!'

Gloria bowed and thanked them and hugged Mark and then left on Tilsbury's arm.

They got a taxi back to Lily's for the night.

'To celebrate Lily's last Christmas,' Tilsbury said softly as they walked through his sister's front door. 'I can't bear for her to be left on her own tonight.'

Chapter 43

Lily looked frail, lying wrapped in blankets on the settee downstairs, next to a roaring log fire.

A real Norwegian fir tree was hung with opulent deep purple, red and gold Christmas decorations and decked with twinkling colourful fairy lights, creating a cosseting, indulging feeling from another era, much like most of the room's furnishings. And the room was so warm they could smell the faint scent of a pine forest.

When she spotted Gloria, Lily held out her hand.

'Hello, dear friend. Come to see me off?' Lily giggled.

'Don't be so melodramatic, Lil,' said Tilsbury. 'I'm just going to make some tea for me and Gloria. Do you want some or more Prosecco?'

Lily pulled a face and held out her slim-stemmed wineglass with a wiggle.

'Have you at least had a nice Christmas, so far, though, love?' Gloria said carefully.

Even though she felt immensely sorry for Lily, Gloria would've preferred Tilsbury to have dropped her back at her own flat, instead of at Lily's house. It was past eleven p.m.

now and Gloria was dog-tired. She wondered where Tilsbury'd got the money from, for the taxi, unless Lily had given it to him.

'It is what it is, Gloria. But I've always liked Christmases in the past. Please hurry up, Tils. Gloria's flagging. We're all flagging. Get the bloody box,' Lily called out to Tilsbury, who was busying himself in the kitchen.

Tilsbury didn't rush back into the room. He came in carefully carrying the tea tray. He set the tray down on the coffee table and poured their tea and topped up Lily's glass with her sparkling wine.

He also took two more glasses off the sideboard behind them and placed them on the table and filled the glasses. He handed one to Gloria.

'Right. Now, I know it's late but I want you to hear me out, love,' he said to Gloria as if Lily wasn't there.

'Well, we're here tonight for two reasons. First of all, we're here to propose a toast to my favourite family member, my dear sister Lily. So I propose a toast for her long, very eventful and happy life, now that this might very well be her, um, last Christmas with us. To my darling sister Lily!'

'To dear Lily!' Gloria said.

Gloria and Tilsbury and Lily clinked glasses. Gloria did not feel comfortable with this proposal but duly sipped her alcohol.

'Oh and you're stayin' tonight by the way, Gloria, to join in with our last family Christmas together. But the second reason I want to have a toast with my two favourite women is the reason I went away . . .'

Gloria looked at him, puzzled, which increased Lily's merriment. Gloria was pleased Lily was tipsy. Perhaps, that way, she wouldn't be thinking about things in too much depth.

'Yes, love?' she said to encourage Tilsbury.

'Ah well. The reason I went away was because you got me thinking about things. The social weren't much help to me. I could be on that list for a long time and maybe I ain't got a long time left. Maybe none of us have. Who knows at our age? But I knew that if I said yes to you – yes to going back and living with you again and all the trouble that is definitely gonna cause with your Cleggy and co – well, I knew I had to do things different this time round. I mean, as you know, I ain't got much by way of possessions and the like but I'd always wanted to go to Scotland. I got a mate up there, too. So, anyway, I did both. Lily gave me the fare and enough for a few nights in a hotel. So I stayed in a nice hotel in Edinburgh and went about a bit to see the sights. Well, after that I thought I needed to do the other thing I went there for – to earn some money –'

'Oh get on with it, Tils, or we'll *all* be goners by the time you finish!' Lily pouted.

'You be quiet, woman! So anyways I walked round a bit, asking after work at some of the hotels, which wasn't forthcoming on account of my age, of course. But finally, I hooked up with my old mate, Dave Brett – you remember him, Glor?

A canny chap from way back. Well, I call him old but he's younger than us.'

Gloria shrugged.

'Well, he was always telling me to come see him. So the next day, I went to see him. His son's got a pub up there. So I asked him if he knew where I could get some temporary work. So he said: well you can work here, old mate! He wasn't bothered about me age, on account he was desperate 'cos some young tike'd let them down. Said this kid was on the sick but then he just pissed off. So they give me the chap's room and basic pay for doing some kitchen portering and glass collecting at nights, up to Christmas. He'd got temps to do the actual Christmas from a hotel agency. But I worked every night and it was real hard graft I can tell you – I was bloody knackered. Them Scots can drink a pint or six, that's for sure. But, anyway, it were cash in hand, no questions asked. So I'm back here now for keeps. And I can't *prove* that I'll never go wanderin' off again, Glor, but trust what I'm saying. I've had plenty of time to think about things now and I know how I want the rest of my life to pan out. So I *am* back for keeps. And the reason I did it was for this.'

Tilsbury took a swig of his tea as he didn't particularly like the fizzy white wine. Then he went to the Christmas tree and retrieved a couple of gifts. He threw one gently at Lily and handed the other to Gloria. Gloria's eyes opened wide.

'But, Tils, you didn't have to do all that just to get me a present, love,' Gloria protested.

'Just open it, Gloria!' Lily smiled, opening her own gift and exclaiming in surprise.

'Oh, Tilsbury! You got it for me! And just in time too! Oh that's marvellous, my love. Come here and give your big old sister a hug!'

Tilsbury allowed himself to be pulled into his sister's embrace for a cosy hug and a sisterly kiss.

'Happy Christmas, Lily, darling!'

Gloria could tell he sounded choked. Well he would do, under the circumstances. It was very upsetting.

'Jasperware!' Lily said proudly. 'I collect it. Okay then – Wedgwood to you and I. But just look how beautiful and smooth this bud vase is! It completes a collection of vases I've got.'

Gloria touched it and smiled. 'It's lovely.'

'Okay then, Gloria, have ya got down to the next layer of gift wrap yet?' Tilsbury said, impatiently.

'Ooo nearly. You've wrapped it well! Mebbe a bit too much sticky tape though!'

The Christmas wrapping finally fell away and the little red box stared at her. Her heart missed a beat.

'So,' Tilsbury was saying. 'The reason I needed to make some serious money quite quickly was so I could say "yes" to yer proposal of me living with you again, *providing you now open that little red box* and say "yes" to what lies inside.'

Gloria lifted the hinged lid of the little red velvet box to reveal a shiny gold engagement ring, set with a sparkling diamond solitaire in the middle.

Gloria gasped. 'It's – it's beautiful, Tilsbury!'

'Well I'm glad you like it, Glor. I chose it because you're a real diamond to me, you see. And the other reason I chose it is because I wanted to do things properly for once; the way we should've done things properly way back in the day. So will ya marry me, Gloria Frensham? I've always loved ya, you know.'

Gloria stared, speechlessly, from the ring to the proud but loving look on Tilsbury's happy face.

'Yay! Cheers to that!' said the excited Lily, downing her Prosecco before the shocked Gloria could open her mouth to reply.

Chapter 44

It was as if time stood still.

The glowing embers of the fire, warming their souls; the Christmas tree with its twinkly lights, making this moment exquisite; Lily's radiant face, having been allowed to join in with this special moment of Tilsbury's, despite her sad illness; wineglasses on tall stems, outstretched towards her, encouraging her response . . .

Clegg would not be amused, of course. Oh, Cleggy. *Whatever happened to you, son!* But this wasn't Clegg's life. The sparkling solitaire, set in a crown of gold on a nine-carat-gold band, beckoned. A smile started on her lips, her cheeks flushing in a blush, as she took the beautiful ring from its box.

Gloria was nodding, as tears of joy started to trickle down her cheeks.

'Oh, I will, Tilsbury, you crazy man! It really is beautiful, love. And I shall. And I ruddy well *do!* I've always loved you, too, Tils. We've always been soul mates, you and I.'

Tilsbury took the ring from her and edged it slowly onto her finger. It was slightly large but could always be re-sized. Gloria got to her feet and hugged Tilsbury for a long time.

Then she went over to the settee and hugged the happy Lily.

And then they laughed and chatted and drank the rest of their wine and the tea went cold and they finally fell asleep in their armchairs.

* * *

Tilsbury gently shook Gloria awake. Ow, her neck was cricked and she still felt tired. Too many bubbles and too many comfy cushions scattered around the place meant they'd ended up sleeping on the floor of the lounge. It wasn't quite as hard as Mabel's floor had been, though.

Lily was softly snoring on the settee. The clock over the mantel read 8.35 a.m. Gloria suddenly remembered the sparkling ring on her finger and looked down to admire it. Her smile reached her eyes, as she also remembered Tilsbury's wonderful proposal from the night before.

'Good morning, future husband.' She grinned.

Tilsbury kissed her nose. 'Good mornin', future wife!' He smiled. 'Right! Now I'm going to make some tea and toast for us all and then can you help me get Lily in the shower? The Macmillan nurses would kill me if they knew I hadn't put her to bed last night. Anyway, she's got Nellie and May coming round for tea this morning and she'll want to be dressed in her finest garb. They'll be here around eleven. So we'll get sorted and I'll leave a pot of tea and biscuits out for them. Then we'll stroll off home. All right? I got our taxi booked for 10.45.'

Gloria nodded that it was quite all right.

Lily took a while to come round but was gracious about being helped in the shower. By eleven Nellie and May were seated in the lounge with a freshly dressed Lily and pot of tea for three waiting on the table. Tilsbury whisked Gloria out of the door before goodbyes became emotional. Gloria said she would ring Lily that evening.

The taxi back to Sheringham was not cheap but Tilsbury was flush for once in his life and did not care about the price.

He even had a small holdall with him, a possession he'd never had before, and a new change of clothes and toiletries.

As they entered the flat he breathed in the air of newness and cleanliness that surrounded them.

'Aye you've done well here, lass. It's a champion place this with no crumblies. Oh and I like the view. And, you're right, we'll be able to do some nice walks, here. Or just sit outside with a cup of tea or summat stronger!' he said, leaning on the handrail of the small balcony. 'Right, so show me what else we've got then? Ooo, a nice new kitchen. And what's in here? Oh yup, that looks like a power shower. Yes I like the bathroom too. And oh wow, you already got me a bed next to yours! Hmm. I can see it's not a double, though . . .'

'Well that was before –'

'Ha, ha. I'm just ribbin' you, darlin'. It's perfect, Gloria. Everything's perfect. Can I kiss you, my lovely?'

Gloria fell into his arms and he kissed her all over her face: little fast, frenzied kisses that had her giggling and finally pushing him off her.

'Gerroff, you great lummox! We'll save all that for later . . . !'

Chapter 45

Tilsbury knew what had happened when they rang Lily, twice, that afternoon and got no response.

She always kept the phone nearby. Just in case. But she'd even refused help from the Macmillan nurses at the very end.

'Just wanna be in my own home amongst the last of my family,' she'd told them, when the taxi arrived to collect her, from hospice, just before Christmas. The nurses knew they couldn't stop her. She'd always been a strong-willed woman. But she'd been told the end of her life was imminent and so they couldn't blame her for wanting to be at home, surrounded by the things and people she loved.

Tilsbury left Gloria to go back to Lily's house and found her, sitting upright, the tea drunk, the biscuits eaten, her dearest friends Nellie and May long gone.

She'd left instructions for what she wanted to happen with her funeral arrangements and all her possessions, after her death, in a letter:

To my dearest brother Tilsbury,

Well, if you're reading this letter you must realise I'm no longer with you. But I'll always be with you and Marvin, Tils, in your hearts.

So, as I know you hate my melodramatics, I'll be brief but I do want to let you know that I've always loved you dearly and I hope you'll find happiness in your own inimitable way. But please be aware that Love will always be the answer to emotional happiness! And with you it has always been Gloria, you oaf!

Took you long enough!

Funeral arrangements: simple funeral, no songs, just the tune from Morning Has Broken, _hummed by a choir. I'd've enjoyed that poignant spectacle whether I'd been dead or alive; it's such a melodic tune. And a prayer of your choice._

Guests: Yourself, Marvin, Jocelyn, Gloria, Nellie and May, if they'll come.

Wedgwood collection: The town museum have expressed an interest, so please give it to them.

House: I've done the paperwork for you to sign it over to the National Trust to sell to increase their coffers.

Furniture, trinkets, jewellery and money in bank accounts: Please use the proceeds of all this stuff for your forthcoming wedding to Gloria and subsequent honeymoon.

Morgan sports car: Please give my car to Marvin to use – if he can squeeze into it (he's got a bit porky of late, ha,

ha) – or to sell or whatever. I've sorted out the relevant
paperwork and he'll know what needs to happen next.

Other than that, dear bro, I'll see you up there, or down
there or wherever 'there' happens to be, later.

Your loving sis, Lil XXX

That was Lily to the end, so organised, he'd thought. But it made all the processes so much easier to deal with.

Tilsbury had held her and cried for a long time before he contacted the Macmillan nurses and let them know what had happened. Both Tilsbury and Gloria were shocked it had happened much sooner than they'd expected.

It was a bright but chilly wintry day with an impishly icy breeze blowing, the morning of Lily's funeral. The vicar's black garb billowed in the wind as he welcomed everyone into the church and said a few words. Gloria had done Lily proud by organising the church to be filled with fragrant white lilies. And the choir brought tears to everybody's eyes. Tilsbury was inconsolable. But Nellie and May both said Lily would have loved the pomp of her own farewell.

Chapter 46

A few days after the funeral, Tilsbury broached the subject of their wedding.

'So we could go for it now or later, love. Or whatever you want.'

'Are you sure you're up to all of this, though, my love? Lily's not long been buried. I don't want you to rush into anything you're not ready for, Tils.'

'Life is very short, Glor. I know that well enough. Lily lived an exuberant life filled with crazy events and lots of love. She wanted that for me too. But my life path has meant it's already taken me a lot longer to get to where I should've been going. And, not knowing how long any of us have got left, Lily was keen for me to get a push-on with the rest of mine. So I *know* I'm ready to do this now.'

Gloria nodded thoughtfully.

'Okay then, ducks. Well my best scenario would be for a spring wedding, here in Sheringham, followed by our honeymoon, later on, in July at that hotel in Eastbourne. That way all my lovely friends can join in. And I'd like Jocelyn and your Marvin to come to Eastbourne, with us, too. But I know they ain't really got the money. So I've been thinking that I'd like to pay for them as a one-off.'

'Well no, my love. I'd like to pay for them, if I may. I owe them big time, don't I? And I have the money to do that for them for once. Anyway, it's only fair. I want to pay my dues and start being responsible for a change. It's a new experience for me, that is!'

Gloria laughed. 'Aye, you're right, there. Well, is that settled then?'

'It is, my love. So we can set them big old wheels in motion.'

'Good, but there's just one more thing that needs doin' before we set a date and it's not goin' to be pleasant!'

* * *

Gloria didn't know how Val had persuaded Clegg to come round for afternoon tea with her and Tilsbury, a few weeks later, but somehow she had. She'd rung Val, beforehand, and told her about Tilsbury's proposal but warned her not to say anything to Clegg for fear of more ruddy reprisals and threats.

'I just can't take all this crap and walking on eggshells all the time with him, Val. So I need to get things in the open, once and for all and then we'll all just live our lives. And if it doesn't suit Cleggy, then it doesn't. Tough shit. But can ya leave it for me to tell him? Might help if you act a bit surprised too. Don't want to get ya into trouble with him, either. Yes, love, of course you and the kids are invited to the wedding and reception. Yes, probably at the Sheringham hotel again. They did us so proud for my eightieth, didn't they, love? Okay great. See you soon.'

The nights were still dark early, of course, being the end of January, so afternoon tea had been decided on instead of having them round for dinner. A light snow was falling on the Sunday they arrived. Val walked in smiling and cheerful, commenting on the spicy buttered scones with jam and cream and egg mayonnaise sandwiches Gloria knew were everybody's favourite.

Clegg was tight-lipped and morose but did manage to squeeze a curt 'Afternoon' out to nobody in particular.

Tea was poured and conversation was kept light until the food was finished and Val helped Gloria take the dishes to the kitchen and load her spanking new dishwasher.

'Mmm nice dishwasher. We could probably do with another one 'cos ours no longer works. I've become the dishwasher again, which is painful after so many years of having one. Ha, ha!' Val commented.

In the lounge Clegg and Tilsbury kept their eyes averted and didn't say a word.

Tilsbury was sure Clegg would soon want to smash his face in, about their recent engagement, but he made sure he didn't smirk or snigger to rile him.

Before Gloria came back and sat down, she opened the small red box and slipped her ring on. When she returned she simply held out her left hand with her new and re-adjusted engagement ring, sitting snugly on her third finger.

Val gasped and dramatically put her hands to her mouth, as they'd agreed she should.

'Oh, Gloria! That is lovely! Oh, congratulations, Tilsbury! Congratulations, Gloria!'

'Well, Cleggy?' Gloria challenged.

Clegg's face had gone puce. Words defied him. But then suddenly they were spewing out of him like a volcanic eruption.

'What the – ? You cannot be serious, Mother! You're eighty years old, for fuck's sake! And you brought me out here for this crazy bloody drama? Have you totally lost your sodding mind? You –'

'BE QUIET, SON. Settle down. How DARE you speak to your mother like that!' bellowed Tilsbury standing up.

'DON'T YOU EVER USE THE WORD "SON" WITH ME, YOU FUCKING SCOUNDREL –'

'But he is,' said Gloria, quietly.

Perhaps it was her demeanour that made everyone suddenly stop – completely stop – and turn and stare at her, completely and utterly shocked, including Tilsbury, who also didn't know.

Ever so quietly, Gloria repeated those startling words.

'TILSBURY is YOUR father. YOU are his SON. Oh and to clear up any further misunderstandings, Arthur knew. It's why he married me when he did. He was a good 'un and I did love him. I loved him throughout our married life, just so you all know.'

Gloria was silent, herself, for a moment. She glanced around the room, noting Val's open mouth and Cleggy's bulging, frightened eyes. In a way, she couldn't believe she'd actually uttered those startling words after so many years. It did, actually, sound preposterous. But it was long overdue admitting.

She then turned to Tilsbury.

'I'm – er – I'm sorry I never told you about this back then, Tils. I'm sure it's a monstrous shock for you. For everyone, in fact. But you were always flitting from one thing to another, in those days, and you were away a lot. I realised you were far too unreliable for fatherhood back then, which is why I never told you. And then you went and married Jocelyn and things got complicated. But that's it! And that's everything! Now, unfortunately, if none of you can deal with this – if none of you wants to try and understand how it was for me back then, being single and pregnant and how these things can just sometimes happen, then I'm sorry. But I've said my piece. And now I'd like you all to just please go home and absorb everything I've said!'

For a moment no one could breathe or move or say anything. They sat rigid, as if time had suddenly stopped, too. But it was only for a moment . . .

Chapter 47

The following March, Gloria's stunning off-white wedding outfit, consisting of a short lace top with three-quarter sleeves and satin skirt was chosen with Val and Jessie on a shopping spree in Norwich. She'd told Tilsbury, earlier, that she intended to choose a simple bouquet of lilies, for her wedding bouquet, in remembrance of his adored sister Lily. They'd also go perfectly with her dress. The feather, net and satin fascinator was Jessie's idea instead of a short veil.

'It's so *in*, Grandma!'

But Gloria had drawn the line at matching high heels of Jessie's choosing and gone for the matching kitten heels, as suggested by Val.

'You wait 'til ya get to my age, ducks,' Gloria warned her granddaughter. 'You'll always go for comfort over high fashion!'

The 'something old' was going to be Joe's beautiful pendant he'd given her in Eastbourne, which reminded her of a very important time in her life; the something new was her lovely wedding attire; something borrowed was a pashmina from Val, in case it got cold; and the something blue was Lily's last parting gift of a hand-stitched, pale blue garter – something she had acquired many moons ago in Sri Lanka.

Val treated them to afternoon tea, afterwards.

They sank into their seats exhausted, shopping bags surrounding them, and gobbled down their delicious sandwiches and scones, bursting with fresh double cream and strawberry jam. It reminded Gloria of the last afternoon tea she'd shared with Tilsbury, seemingly a lifetime ago, in the park gardens. Yet it was less than a year ago.

'C'mon, Gran. I want a picture of us three ladies before I shoot off to meet my mates!' said Jessie, getting her iPad ready and handing it to the waitress. 'You sit in the middle, Gran.'

It brought a tear to Gloria's eye to realise how she'd been fully accepted back into her old family, even though that clearly wasn't the case, yet, with Clegg.

Jessie kissed them afterwards and left.

'So, now we're alone, how *is* Clegg these days?'

Val let out a long whistle. 'Well, after he lost it back at your place, when you informed him about his, let's say, unrealised parentage and they – um – carted him off to the Marley Institution –'

'*He smashed up my new place, is what he did, Val, and terrified us all, which is why I called the police!*' Gloria shot back, furious at the very thought.

Val grimaced but reached out and rubbed Gloria's arm. 'God, I know, Gloria. It's okay. It was bloody awful. We were all very shocked that day. And I know it still hurts. But, in fact, in a strange way I'm glad this all happened. Something had been brewing with him for years. Your confession was the icing on his cake. And I think it came out at just the right time.'

Gloria shook her head, dismissively, at this.

'So anyway,' Val continued, 'the people in the institute tried to tackle what was going on with him. But he just wouldn't answer them; wouldn't speak to them at all, in fact. Then I was asked to give my version of events and they said they'd try residential counselling to see what that'd reveal. But all they got was abuse, with him shouting and swearing at them. He just wouldn't open up at all. So a few weeks later they told me the next thing they were going to try was putting him on a low sedation dose and try to get him to open up without all the hysterics. By the end of that first month, I was summoned to see them. The counsellor said he'd finally opened up a little and what he told her was, that he'd felt as a man, he should never talk about his problems and so he'd been bottling things up all his life.'

Gloria scowled at this comment.

'Anyway, the upshot is that he says he never wanted to be an army man. It was just an easy option when he left school. Apparently Arthur'd said he didn't want him wastin' his life, hanging round the council estate, like the other lads. He also says he hates his current job but he doesn't know how to go about changing it now he's in his mid-fifties. He wanted to retire early in order to escape his problems but we don't have any money put aside for that.

'So he tried to tell me that if we could get you out of your house you'd probably help us out putting the kids through uni with a bit left over for ourselves as well as enough to pay for putting you in a home eventually. At the same time he could see that you were going downhill too and he just didn't know how to cope with that, on top of everything else. This is why he was venting his anger on all of us but especially, unfortunately, on you. He said it felt like his whole world was collapsing. And then, of course, finding out that Tilsbury was his birth father was just another challenge he couldn't deal with and so it pushed him completely over the edge.'

'Oh charming! Not man enough to face up to things, is it?'

'No, Gloria,' Val said softly. 'Not coherent enough to ask for help when he was failing and falling. Mental health's becoming quite an issue these days. I see this kind of thing a lot in my job, especially with men. I feel terrible that I didn't notice the signs. I guess, sometimes, you don't see what's right under your nose. But I get it now. And, talking to the counsellor, she suggested it would help him if we all tried to pull together on this and help him sort things out. I do still love him, you see. And I don't want to split up over this. In fact, I don't want any of us to split up over this. I think we can find a way to work through this. I think you and I have found friendship and the kids adore you. We want you back in our lives. But, on the other hand, we don't want to be in the middle of a war between you and Cleggy all the time.'

'Well yes, that's all very well, ducks. And I'm glad you're standing by him and all. It's just that he's put me through the mill. And I've had a skinful. At eighty, you'd expect life to get easier, love. Not more stressful.'

Val nodded. 'I know, Gloria. So I'm hopeful they'll sort something out and things might just start looking up. They've said he can come home for a couple of days, occasionally. It's supposed to break him back into his own environment, gently, and see how it goes from there. Then they'll reassess him again later.'

'Well, let's wait and see what happens with that then, shall we, love?'

'We shall, yes. I'll keep in touch with you, anyways. I'm sorry about all this, Gloria. I really am,' said Val, sighing inwardly, then standing up and wrapping her arms around Gloria for a long hug.

Chapter 48

Church organ music always made Gloria feel sad.

To her, it never seemed to be played accompanied by violins, trumpets or any other accoutrements of pleasure. They were never cheerful or foot-tapping tunes. Whatever the occasion, the melody always seemed to be serious, dull or melancholy. But the one sombre tune she was thrilled to hear as she entered the church on Jocelyn's arm, in the middle of April, for her own wedding to Tilsbury that day, was the wedding march: *Here Comes the Bride (Processional)* by Richard Wagner.

Tears graced her eyes as she looked at Jocelyn, pretty in a pale blue outfit, with her hair done especially for Gloria's important occasion.

They hugged briefly as Gloria whispered, 'You *sure* you're okay about this, though, ducks?'

'Oh, of course, you old trout,' Jocelyn whispered back with a grin. 'I got me Marvin now and we're happy, love. Tils never was really mine, as we both know. C'mon now watch your mascara. Right. Nice and ready now?'

Just as Gloria braced herself and started to take her first steps down the aisle, someone tapped her on the shoulder.

'Could I cut in?' said a familiar but odd-sounding voice. Gloria was trying to place it as she turned round to see Clegg, smartly dressed in a suit, with the same corsage as the rest of the wedding party.

Gloria stopped and stared, her mouth falling open in utter shock. 'What the 'eck are you –'

'I'm giving my mother away to be married. Well, I've been working up to this moment with the institute's help and my lovely Val as well of course. And, naturally, the kids wanted me to "get my act together and stop hurtin' everyone," they said. Can't say I'm always gonna be perfect, now, Mother, but I'm gettin' there. And this, this is part of it. It – well – it was my idea, actually. You might not believe that. But when I mentioned it to Jessie, she was thrilled. She adores you. They both do. And I do actually want to do this for you today as well, Mum. So it's not just an act or summat.

'I've been a twat, I'll grant you that. But now I understand stuff I never understood before. The people at the institute, um, opened my eyes to things. And I also know you love Tilsbury and I'm fine with that. I wasn't at first, of course. Understandably, it was a ruddy great big shock, it was. But I've, er, worked through most of my problems and I'm okay about this now. I promise,' he said quietly.

Gloria searched his eyes for the mania that was there the last time she looked. There was no way her wedding was going to be spoiled by further hysterics. But Val came up to them.

'Please don't worry, Gloria. He's not going to ruin anything. He really wants to do this. They made him see sense at the institute, like with you at the nursing home. And, pretty much like you at Green's, they seem to have got through most of the barriers. He understands us all a lot better now. He understands himself more too. I'm sorry Jocelyn. Do you mind if we do this?'

Jocelyn shrugged. She did mind and she had plenty to say about it *and them* for hurting her best friend over the years. But today was neither the time, nor was this the place. So she kept a lid on her feelings and went back to her seat, next to Marvin, muttering. Marvin grinned at her and took hold of her hand.

'You knew about this?' she hissed at him.

'It's okay, love. It's sortin' itself out is what it's doin'.'

The music played on and Gloria began to walk slowly down the aisle. Clegg's arm was firm. It felt okay. Maybe it would be okay. She'd had Val's reassurance. But Clegg was the *last person* she ever expected to see guiding her towards her happy union with Tilsbury.

'She's all yours, mate,' said Clegg, genially when he got to where Tilsbury was proudly surveying Gloria in her beautiful wedding dress. 'And thanks for doing that other thing. I'm very grateful,' he added with a wink and then walked back slowly to join Val.

'What's he mean?' Gloria whispered to Tilsbury. But Tilsbury just winked at her, smiled and took Gloria's arm.

'Let's just get married, my love, like we should've done a long time ago.'

* * *

Gloria was thrilled that Joe and Vittori and the girls, Florence, Freda and Dot had been able to come along. They were all her new best friends now.

'Well you never know when yer number's up, Gloria. Gotta make the most of life, don't you, love,' said Dot, holding on to Florence's arm. 'Gives the rest of us hope, though, when we see how you've turned *your* life around from what it was like.'

'I treated myself to a new dress for your wedding!' Freda smiled, giving the pale lemon chiffon dress a twirl.

'And we'll all be at the hotel on yer honeymoon, as usual, like you said you hoped for. Hope you don't really mind all us rabble joining in with you on your special holiday, though,' said Florence grinning.

Joe had taken Gloria to one side. 'I'm really pleased you included my necklace as your something old, Gloria. You do look beautiful today, I must say,' said Joe, dabbing at his own eyes. He said he had a speck of dust in them.

'It was perfect as my something old, Joe. Thank you for treating me in the first place. And how are you doing these days, anyway?'

'Much better since meeting you, Gloria. You're always so upbeat. Put a bit of a spring in my step, it has. Plus, well, I'm starting to get used to the fact that there's a bit more life for me now my Carol's passed. It's not the same without her, though. Not as fulfilling. But I can see that one can exist and have a few laughs from time to time while you, um, while you wait for that other day . . . And I've been asked to join our local Sudoku team, full-time.'

Gloria smiled broadly and kissed him on the cheek. 'Ah, well that's great, Joe. That's great news. I always think as long as you've got summat to look forward to then there's a reason to carry on. Good for you. And how are you Vittori?'

'I very happy to be here. Very warm and inviting. Like the Italians. And you very pretty lady,' Vittori said, raising his glass. 'And very nice foods.'

The buffet the Sheringham hotel had put on for their wedding luncheon was indeed very nice and even surpassed the one they put on for Gloria's eightieth birthday party.

Gloria was relieved that Cleggy had behaved himself, as he and Val had promised. She walked over to him and clinked glasses with them both.

'Well this is a far cry from the state of play a few months back. Wouldn't you say so, son?' she said.

She noted that Val nudged Cleggy's arm.

'Well, yes it is, Mother. I guess we thought it was only going to be YOU that we sorted out. Then turns out it was a problem *I* probably created for us all.'

Gloria nodded. 'Probably was a bit of both. We're a very proud family, I suppose.'

'Aye we are that. But, um, talking of proud . . . I have to say that I'm, er, I'm very proud of you today, too, Mother. I really can't believe your incredible turnaround. I thought, in a way, we were finished as a family. And I know that's a strong thing to say. But I couldn't cope back then and I thought you couldn't either. So I thought there was no way back for either of us. But you're built of sterner stuff than I am, Mother; I will say that. And just look at you now. You're married. You've found a lovely new home. Our kids adore you. Oh and I can't wait to be introduced properly to all your very lovely new friends.'

Tears misted Gloria's eyes. 'Well, I'm thrilled you think so, Cleggy. Now come here. About time we had a bit of a hug, isn't it, son. That's one of the things I've most wanted out of all this. A bit of love and acceptance from you.'

But it was Clegg who reached out to her first, without Val nudging him, and he drew Gloria into a tight hug.

Chapter 49

Tears bubbled in Tilsbury's eyes as he clinked champagne glasses with Gloria, after they'd eaten their fill at the buffet table. He looked so smart in his new wedding suit that Gloria had fallen in love with him all over again. They'd had the first dance, care of Malcolm, the pub singer who'd crooned Tilsbury's favourite Elvis Presley song, 'Can't Help Falling in Love'.

'So how does it feel to no longer be Mrs Frensham, eh, Mrs Hunter?' Tilsbury had whispered.

'It actually feels quite wonderful, Mr Hunter. Mmm, Gloria Hunter. Got a rather nice ring to it, hasn't it?'

'How ya doin', bruv?' said Marvin, coming up behind Tilsbury and mock punching him.

'Really good, thanks, mate!'

'Shoulda done this years ago but you did like pissin' yer life up against the wall, back then.'

'Well cheers for that fond me'mry, Marv. By the way, I've got summat for you later.'

'Oh yeah? A fight out back over summat?'

'No, you daft oaf. Just summat needs sorting is all.'

'Catch you later then. Just goin' for a walk down the front with Jocelyn to ease me waistline after all that good grub.'

Gloria was talking to her grandchildren in a corner. The cut of Jessie's turquoise dress was perfect, set against her long dark hair. A proper little stunner she was now, Gloria thought, as she handed her the envelope.

'W-what's this gran?' Jessie said slowly.

She handed a similar envelope to the surprised Adam.

Gloria looked into her granddaughter's eyes. Fiercely stubborn when she wanted something, yet as proud as her father, the inimitable Clegg. Gloria even saw herself in her.

'I'm giving you and Adam a lump sum of £15,000 each. I did tell you something would be forthcoming from me when I sold me house. What you do with it's up to yourselves. There's loads of worthwhile things you could do with it, like put a deposit on your first home or whatever. Although if you buy yourselves nice houses, don't go cluttering them up like I did. Ha, ha. Oh and I was hoping, though, Adam, that you might want to put yours towards that Sport and Exercise Management degree course you wanted to do at uni. But like I said, it's up to yourselves. It gives you both a little start in life, like my family did for me and Arthur by leaving us their house. So this is just me giving you both a little summat for your futures, if you choose to use it for that. But no pressure.'

Jessie had tears in her eyes. She opened her arms to Gloria and Adam crept inside that hug too. The three of them stood like that for a while and Gloria realised she couldn't be any happier than she was at that very moment in time.

Gloria left the surprised youngsters discussing what just happened.

'So what were you and Cleggy talking about in the church then, Tils?'

Tilbury looked sheepish.

'Did you know they can have visitors at that Marley's place? Well I spoke to Val and went up with her one day, to see Cleggy, when I thought the time might be right. Just thought I'd try summat, Glor. Wasn't sure we'd ever get on, me and Clegg, after all our bad history. And I still can't get over the shock of knowing that he's mine. *Seems bloody unreal*, in fact. But it is what it is and we've put all that to rest now, haven't we, love. So anyways before I went to see him, I had a chat with the manager here and you know how Val's talking about sellin' up and downsizing and moving nearer to us, somewhere outside Sheringham, once the kids are sorted with the rest of their education and whatnot? Well I thought I'd see if Charlie, here, might just have a bit of pot washing and glass collecting here on the weekends for Cleggy to do. Start him off on a different tack and getting him to mix with folk instead of workin' by himself.'

'What? My Cleggy a pot washer? Have *you* lost the bloody plot now, Tils?' Gloria retorted, pulling away from him.

Tilsbury giggled at her indignation.

'Nah. But it did all right for me in Edinburgh and paid for

most of our weddin' and all, didn't it. Anyway, it's just a start. Get him out of himself a bit. Mixing with lots of different people, you know, as well as him tryin' summat new. Like the rest of us,' Tilsbury explained. 'Anyways, Charlie seemed to think it'd work for them. Plus he reckoned if Cleggy proved himself by working in the kitchen, he might be promoted to working in the bar or on front of house. He'd get to mix with lots more people then. Plus he'd have a new career to boot, in catering, if that's what he decided he wanted to do!'

Gloria shook her head. But just at that moment Val and Clegg approached them.

'Here, Cleggy. Sorry about Tilsbury trying to get you a job here. I didn't know he'd got in touch with Charlie, here. Sorry love.'

'No, it's all right, Mum. And Val thinks it's a wonderful idea, too. Just to ease me back into things – and it's a completely different kind of job. You might not think it worthy. But it's still a job that somebody has to do, isn't it? Plus you never know what might lead on from it.'

Gloria looked uncertain but shrugged, anyway. 'Yeah, well I suppose. Like you say, it could be a new start of sorts. Adam tells me you gave up work at your old company. Did you?'

'I did, Mother. They gave me a nice little payoff for all the years I put in, so that's something. But I felt I couldn't go back there. I think it was the start of most of my problems you see. I couldn't take the stress. Anyway, I think it's very kind of Tilsbury to think of me. Stops me sittin' and mopin' at home. And one day we might just move to these parts. It's lovely here. Not stressful at all. We'd fancy something like a two-bed cottage on the outskirts, subject to us sellin' ours in the future, of course.'

'Yeah, we all fancy that idea, Gloria.' Val smiled. 'It'd be a complete change for us. Because I think we're ready to face up to some changes, now, with the kids on the verge of movin' out and the rest. Plus we'd be near to you if you ever got in the position where you'd *need* us to be near to you. And please, please forget your worry about us putting you into an old people's home at some point later in the day. We know you don't want that and neither do we, love, so it won't be happening. When the time comes we'll get you a carer, or we can look at other options to help you both to continue living in your own new home. Oh and, er, thank you SO much for the kids' envelopes. They were completely gobsmacked. And Adam *will* be using his for uni.'

'Yes thanks, Mum,' Clegg cut in. 'Thanks for everything. I've been a twat. Sorry. My life was collapsin' before. But I think I'm on the right road now, thanks to you and, um, thanks to Tilsbury as well.'

Jocelyn came rushing over to Gloria, showering her with hugs and kisses.

'Cor thanks, Glor. Thanks from the bottom of me heart for your gift of a holiday. Thanks, Tils, old fruit. You're a star! And yes, we do accept this lovely gift. Can't get over it, actually, love. Didn't think we'd ever get there. All that talk about holidays and I was thinking we'll never be able to afford it! And now we can and especially on yer honeymoon, which will be totally amazin', my lovelies. Just can't wait and it'll be so much fun. Just like the good old days.'

Gloria then picked up a spoon and banged it on a stainless steel serving bowl to get everybody's attention.

'Right, everyone, well me and Tils are toddling off home now. We've done what we came to do. We love you all lots and want you to stay and have fun. But we're tired now. You can only party for so long at eighty, you know. But, anyways, c'mon, ladies! Get together. I'm gonna throw me bouquet. Oh crikey! Don't know if I can throw it backwards like you see people doin'.'

'Just chuck it, Glor!' shouted Jocelyn.

Tilsbury steadied her as she turned with her back to the wedding party. She bent forward and then launched her arm backwards in the air.

There was a little gasp when someone caught her bouquet. Gloria turned to see who'd caught it.

Florence. 'Oh my! *Oh my*! They're lovely! But I haven't had a man in YEARS!' Florence blushed.

'Well, you're not missin' much!' someone quipped.

'Best get a move on then, love!' joked someone else.

Gloria and Tilsbury marched out of the door, amidst raucous laughter and cheering, as confetti and rice were chucked over them by the bucket-load.

Chapter 50

Blue skies with wispy, fluffy clouds and a turquoise sea welcomed the recent newly-weds, Gloria and Tilsbury, as well as Jocelyn and Marvin, as they arrived at the Eastbourne hotel, on their late shared honeymoon cum holiday. It was a deliciously warm twenty-two degrees for the middle of July.

'Cor, will ya look at that sea, Joss!' exclaimed Marvin. 'Quite a diff'rent colour to the Ganges, that's for sure. Eh, bruv?'

'Aye, it is that, Marv,' said Tilsbury. 'It's a cracker. And I think this place could grow on me. Well, let's go get settled in, folks. Then we'll hit the prom and find a nice boozer someplace, eh?'

That evening they enjoyed a cracking celebratory party, care of Lily's wedding money she'd bequeathed them. Most of the usual crowd were there for the happy couple's special celebrations, which thrilled Gloria, and she spent half the night introducing everybody.

'Great to see you folks again.' Joe grinned, shaking hands with the four of them.

'*Buonasera*, Mrs Hunter!' said Vittori, breaking off from chatting to Florence, and raising his glass to them.

'Hello! Hello, Gloria! Oh but you give us something to look forward to, each time we meet,' said Dot.

'Yeah,' said Jocelyn. 'Well, that's our Gloria for ya. Grass don't grow under her feet. That's for sure!'

Gloria loved catching up with everyone's news, especially the ones who hadn't made it to her eightieth or her wedding. And there was lots of laughter and jokes about Gloria getting married again at her 'time of life'. She handed out photos of both her celebrations.

At the end of that night and before anyone else actually fell asleep at their table, as one old lady had, Gloria and Tilsbury were presented with one large card, signed by everyone, both for Gloria's eightieth and their wedding, with hundreds of tiny shiny gold star-shaped sprinkles inside the card, which ended up all over the floor in the restaurant.

'Thank you! Thank you, everybody! Thank you so much for your kind wishes!' said Gloria. 'See? I told you I'd be back!'

'Yes but we didn't think it would be for your *honeymoon*, old girl!'

Everybody'd roared with laughter.

'You're mad, bad people, you four, you are!' said someone. 'But you sure know how to party. Come back, any time!'

'Can't actually remember the last time I had this much fun, Glor!' said Jocelyn, grinning ear to ear. 'Well this won't be *our* last time in Eastbourne, either, once Marv sells Lily's car that he can't ruddy get into, the fat sod!'

There were a few sore heads, at breakfast, the next day.

'Ooo, can't be doin' this at my time of life,' Jocelyn admitted, laughingly. 'Hurts too much!'

But then Florence appeared with sad news that Freda had suddenly taken ill and been rushed into hospital. Florence, who was close friends with Freda and always shared rooms with her on holiday, had dialled 999, then rang Freda's son, Michael. He said he was coming down as soon as. Freda was said to be stable at the hospital but no one actually knew what was wrong with her. She hadn't been suffering with anything serious as far as anyone knew.

On the sightseeing trip around Eastbourne, later that morning, Gloria was feeling a little out of sorts.

'I do feel a bit guilty, about things, though. Hope our partyin' hasn't upset Freda's system or anything. Someone says they're keepin' her in for a few days to do some tests before they let her go home with Michael. He's gone back home for now because he's in the middle of something important at work. But he's coming back at the weekend to see what's what.'

'Yeah, Glor, but at our age ANYTHING could happen, at any time and for any reason! It's got to be expected. She wouldn't be in hospital for a hangover, though, Glor. So it can't've been our party,' reasoned Jocelyn. 'Must've been summat more serious or what they call an underlyin' problem.'

'That's right! Leave it to Joss to dampen the mood,' said Marvin, shooting her a 'shut-your-mouth' glance.

'Yeah but she's right though, Marv,' said Gloria. 'Like I keep sayin', you've got to grab what's left of life now and enjoy every turn. We always need summat to look forward to. Anyways, what do you think, new husband?'

Tilsbury could be heard snoring lightly, in his seat.

'Bloody hell, bruv! Are we all that borin'?'

'Gawd, ducks. Is this what I have to contend with from now on? Him fallin' asleep every time he sits down? Think I want a divorce!' Gloria chuckled.

* * *

The shock about Freda taking ill, however, had turned into mass relief when everybody discovered, later that day, that she'd actually choked on one of her tablets earlier that morning, and then passed out, gasping for breath. She hadn't drunk enough water with it. So – okay – thankfully it hadn't been anything serious on this occasion but her son was driving all the way back down to Eastbourne again, the following morning, to take her back home from the hospital.

'He says he's taking her home to rest after all her excitement. Least he can keep an eye on her that way,' Florence explained.

Michael had to return with Freda to the hotel to collect the rest of her things. She also wanted to say cheerio to all her friends before she went home. She'd waved them all a sad goodbye, from her son's car, because she couldn't finish her holiday with them on this occasion.

'Ta-ra, love! See you next time!' said Florence, who'd helped her son pack her suitcase and get her ready for the off. Joe and Vittori stood next to her, waving goodbye to her friend.

'Bye, everyone!'

'Bye, Freda!'

It was a shame to see her go. But she was in the most caring of hands to be going back home with her loving son.

Yet Gloria knew that every time someone in their age group 'took ill' or had a fall or didn't turn up on holiday, they all realised that, hey, *there but for the grace of God go I*. That final curtain call could happen at any time, to any one of them. Luckily, it hadn't happened to Freda on this holiday. Nor to any of her other new-found friends. Yet.

It was indeed a sad, sobering thought. However, it tightened Gloria's resolve to make sure her final days – whether she had a few months or many years – would be as fulfilled as possible.

* * *

On the last day of their friends' holidays in Eastbourne, and as they were struggling up the steps into the coach for their journeys back home, Gloria and her entourage were standing on the pavement, waving them off.

'The key to all this, like Florence once said, is to just keep taking small steps forward. It gets you through life. And you do always need to have summat exciting to look forward to. Like holidays in Eastbourne!' Gloria said brightly.

'Yeah, me and Marv are with you on that score,' agreed Jocelyn, linking arms with her oldest and best friend.

The coach revved its engine.

'See youse all next year, if any of us make it. Ha, ha!' yelled Gloria.

'Yay, Gloria!' they all shouted back, waving.

'It's a date, love!' Florence grinned, as she boarded with Vittori.

'See you then!' said Dot, waving madly.

'I'll be here every year, while I can,' Joe enthused, giving Gloria, then Jocelyn, a hug, just before he boarded the coach.

Gloria, Tilsbury, Jocelyn and Marvin felt bereft as they carried on waving until the coach was out of sight. They were treating themselves and staying on in the hotel in Eastbourne until the end of the week.

But already it didn't feel the same without everybody else.

Chapter 51

Gloria, Jocelyn, Tilsbury and Marvin sat in their canvas chairs, all in a row, along the edge of the sea with their toes in the cold turquoise water. Marvin and Tilsbury had a little hip flask each of liquor, which they were sipping. Gloria and Jocelyn both had tea, in polystyrene cups from the kiosk up top, although Gloria could smell something slightly stronger than teabags in Jocelyn's.

'S'unbelievable, ain't it, really,' said Gloria. 'All this for us to enjoy!' she said, plonking her cup in the shingle and stretching her tanned arms wide. Today was a very civil twenty-one degrees and a light wind was blowing across the sea, causing sparkling ripples. A lone seagull soared overhead.

'It is, Glor. Bloody unbelievable. But bloody marvellous, too, thanks to you and Tils,' admitted Marvin. 'Well, you know that me, Tils and Lily used to travel a lot with Father, all over India, back in the day. But once we all settled down back here we didn't do it no more. Never went anywhere exotic. Didn't really even do holidays apart from a few days here and there at Great Yarmouth or whatever. And I never truly thought owt could ever be as nice as this holiday, here, with all you rabble. Even more amazin' is that there's actually stuff to look forward to now, at our time of life. You and Tils have opened our eyes to that, Glor. I hope Freda's gonna be all right, though. She didn't look too well, did she, even though we were told she's gonna be all right now?'

'I think she'll be okay. She's lucky she's got a loving family. Not everyone has. Wake Tils up, would you, Marv. What's up with him these days? Or what's he got in that hip flask? Can't have him kippin' like this all the ruddy time. And it's sacrilegious on a lovely day like today!'

'He's obviously gettin' too comfortable with all this marriage malarkey, Glor! Or you've been keepin' him up all night!' Jocelyn laughed.

'I'll wake the git,' said Marvin, shoving Tilsbury.

But it didn't waken him. So Marvin shoved him hard enough that his chair overturned and deposited Tilsbury into the chilly sea. Well *that* woke him.

'Chuffin' hell, guys!' he cried, jumping up, splashing about soaked.

He scrunched his eyes up, a mischievous grin suddenly spreading from ear to ear. 'Right . . . !'

He lurched forward, pushing them all off their chairs, one by one, including Gloria, tipping them straight into the sea. Each one of them squealed equally with delight as well as shock, as their relaxed, yet fully clothed bodies hit the icy water.

'Tilsbury! Stop!' Jocelyn yelled.

Gloria was giggling, uncontrollably. She knew, first-hand, just how cold the sea could be, even in the summer. She remembered their amazing, crazy swim in the North Sea many months ago.

'Crazy effin' bastard!' yelped Marvin, swinging a light-hearted punch at him.

'What?' said Tilsbury. 'I'm living life, like I dunno what tomorrow's gonna bring, you oaf. Well, that's what me new wife keeps tellin' me to do. So get yer lardy arse into this sea right now, bruv! We're swimming to France!'

Acknowledgements

The art of writing takes years of practice, diligence and a few knock-backs. It is a solitary pursuit of excellence and without its supporting cast, who play a major role in our lives, most writers would never realise their dreams of success.

So my thanks go to my editor, the terrific Katie Loughnane, for her upbeat support and dedication, and to all her fantastic colleagues at Avon, HarperCollins.

My thanks also go to my husband Chris, for cups of tea at 4am and his unerring optimism.

If you loved *The Woman Who Kept Everything*, why not try some other Avon books that are guaranteed to lift your spirits and make you smile?

Turn the page for some hand-picked recommendations...

Sometimes we find happiness where we least expect it…

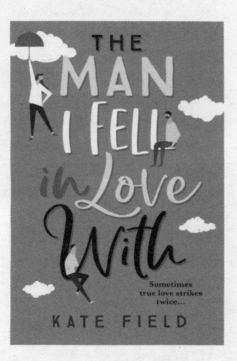

A wonderfully uplifting novel full of wisdom, spirit and charm – this is a love story with a difference...

**Meet Lucy, aged 25, and Brenda, aged 79.
Neighbours, and unlikely friends...**

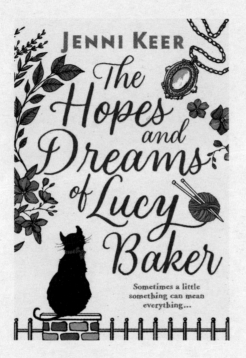

A charming, heart-warming and feel-good novel!